D0504111

THE
NUBBLER

THE
NUBBLER

PAM AYRES

Orion
Children's Books

First published in Great Britain in 1997
by Orion Children's Books
a division of the Orion Publishing Group Ltd
Orion House
5 Upper St Martin's Lane
London WC2H 9EA

Text copyright © Pam Ayres 1997
Illustrations copyright © Caroline Crossland 1997

The right of Pam Ayres and Caroline Crossland
to be identified as the author and illustrator
respectively of this work has been asserted.

All rights reserved. No part of this publication may be
reproduced, stored in a retrieval system, or transmitted,
in any form or by any means, electronic, mechanical, photocopying,
recording or otherwise, without the prior permission
of Orion Children's Books.

A catalogue record for this book is available
from the British Library
Typeset by Deltatype Ltd, Birkenhead, Merseyside
Printed in Great Britain by Butler & Tanner Ltd, Frome and London

ISBN 1 85881 435 9 (hb)

EAST SUSSEX					
V	W&S	INV No. 4112039			
SHELF MARK	JF				
COPY No.	01860884				
BRN	63588				
DATE 5/97	LOC HCJ	LOC	LOC	LOC	LOC	LOC
COUNTY LIBRARY					

CHAPTER ONE

Downstairs his parents raged. Rufus could hear their furious, shouting voices, his father's loud and blunt like a club, and his mother's high, jabbering, the way it always went before she burst into tears, before his father stormed out of the house.

Rufus was curled into a tight ball in the bed. His hands were over his ears but he could still hear perfectly well. Their voices were too savage, too enraged to be shut out by hands. They were rowing about money, or how late his father came home, or about other matters which he only half under-stood.

Rufus's heart pounded in his chest like a drum. Despair and fear of the worst kind roared through him, fear of losing his mum and dad, of being sent reeling into some wasteland where they did not figure. On the chair beside his bed sat a teddy bear with a bow tie. Once he had clung to it for comfort on nights like these but now he didn't bother. Now he recognised it for what it was, just an outgrown toy. Like him it was powerless.

He heard some shouted remark from his father, some cruel parting shot, and the house shook as the front door was

1

violently slammed. Rufus heard the car start and the sound of it being driven off madly, furiously, out of the small modern close where they lived, and into the night. He felt a new gash of fear as he pictured his father driving like that, dangerous, out of control.

Rufus propped himself urgently up on one elbow, listening intently to the movements of his mother downstairs. Was she leaving? Getting out like she always said she would, putting on her coat, scooping her long hair up out of the collar? He got out of bed and went silently to the top of the stairs, peering down through the white banisters.

She was in the sitting-room. She was not moving about. He heard her sniff once, twice. She would be crying in there, crying into a screwed-up tissue, hunched up in her chair the same as always.

Rufus waited in his T-shirt, his thin bare legs ice cold. He hesitated, not knowing what to do. He wanted to rush down to see her of course, to comfort her and be comforted himself, but he didn't go. Not now he was bigger. He had done in the past, rushed down, tried to put his arms round her. She just kept saying how sorry she was, sorry, sorry, he didn't deserve it. He knew now that running downstairs upset her even more.

It was better if she thought he had not heard, if she believed he had slept soundly through the storm. Some chance. Now he stood tense and silent on the landing. After a while he gave up and went quietly back to bed. He curled up, hugging his frozen legs, hating the feel of the house, the bitter words that still hung in the air, the fear of it all starting up again when his father eventually came home.

Rufus did not start to cry until he remembered his English homework. This was Monday night and it was supposed to be ready for Tuesday. He hadn't done it. Realising this with a shock, he sat up. In the dim light he could see the two exercise books untouched on the table beside his computer. Rufus stared at them in alarm and disbelief. He hadn't written the long essay, hadn't even thought about it.

All evening a terrible silent rage had built between his parents, until the atmosphere in the ordinary pleasant little house was charged and flowing with poison. The furious row, when it broke, was almost a relief. But it was no place to write an essay. Essays never even came into it.

Rufus let himself slowly lie back. His stomach churned. He stared up at the ceiling, knowing he was going to be in trouble. Their usual English teacher was off sick and tomorrow the Head of English was taking them, first lesson. People said he was amazingly strict. Rufus would be the only one in the whole class who hadn't done his homework.

He heard a car and tensed in case it was his father returning, but the drone of the engine intensified and then faded away.

He did not know where his father was. Downstairs on her own his mother cried. His homework wasn't done. Every single thing was wrong. A giant sense of unfairness swept over him, he felt tears well up in his eyes and overflow, great buckets of hot tears that ran down the sides of his face into the hair round his ear. Rufus, who had never felt so alone, turned, covered his face in the darkness and shook with long silent sobs.

Into the room there came a faint resinous smell. At first he did not feel the little, hard hand that closed over his.

'Hello,' said the Nubbler.

Rufus looked through his fingers. There was something sitting on the floor beside his bed.

3

'Who are you?' he asked.

'The Nubbler.'

'What do you want?'

'I heard you crying.'

'How?'

'On the headset.'

'*What*?'

Rufus propped himself up on one elbow. There was a thing beside his bed. It wasn't a frightening thing but it was like no thing he had ever seen before.

In the light that came in from the crack around the door he could make out a creature. It looked like ... well, it looked like a dragon, or a big dog, but not really like either. It had a long nose, big shortsighted-looking eyes and skin covered in leafy scales. Round its neck there was a black headset. It sat on the floor beside his bed, filling the room with a sweet woody smell like a fir cone, or a Christmas tree, and it was holding his hand.

Rufus looked down at the small hand. It was webbed between the fingers.

'What do you want?' he asked again.

'I've come to help you along for a bit,' said the Nubbler.

'What d'you mean?'

'Well, it's not very good here, is it?'

'Yes it is!' Rufus said shirtily, defensive because he knew you weren't supposed to talk to just anybody about your mum and dad arguing. It was private, something you were supposed to keep to yourself.

'Oh come on Rufus,' the Nubbler said, 'it's all right. I know all about it. I know your dad's gone off and your mum's down there upset.'

'How do you know?' Rufus asked in a whisper.

4

'Oh, the headset,' said the Nubbler, waving a hand vaguely. 'Anyway, it's all right now, I'll help you along for a bit.'

'Where've you come from?' asked Rufus.

The Nubbler seemed rather evasive and gestured towards the window. 'Oh ... out there. You know. Past the trees.'

'On your own? Did you walk? How did you get here?'

'Mmmm, well, you know. It didn't take long ...'

A possibility was gradually dawning on Rufus. 'Are you magic?' he said slowly.

The Nubbler shrugged and mumbled in a modest, self-deprecating sort of way.

A pure, golden vision of an idea came to Rufus. His heart filled with hope. Urgently he asked 'Can you make my mum and dad stop arguing?'

'No,' said the Nubbler firmly.

'Not at all?'

'No.'

'Well, what can you do then?' asked Rufus, disappointed.

'Well, I'll just give you a shove.'

'What good's that going to do?' asked Rufus, not at all sure that he wanted a shove.

'Oh, you'd be surprised,' said the Nubbler. 'That's all you need, Rufus. A bit of a shove. In the right direction.'

'Rufus?' It was his mother's voice.

She was coming up the stairs. Rufus gasped. He didn't know what the Nubbler was, but he wanted to protect him.

'It's my mother! She'll see you. Hide, quick! Where're you going to go?'

The Nubbler, still holding his hand, said calmly, 'It's all right, Rufus. You don't have to worry. She can't see me.'

5

Rufus was agitated. 'Of course she can see you! You're not *invisible!*'

The Nubbler looked patiently at Rufus with his big kind eyes.

'Yes I am, Rufus. If I want to be, I am.'

He moved out of the way of the door as she softly opened it.

'Are you all right Rufus?' His mother's voice sounded thick and nasal.

Rufus was confused. 'Yes. Yes, I'm all right.'

'Only I thought I heard you talking to somebody.'

Rufus could see the Nubbler at the end of his bed, peering thoughtfully up at his mother. It was true. Incredibly, she *could not* see him.

'No. I'm all right. I had a dream.'

'Did you hear anything ... I mean earlier on?'

'No. I didn't hear anything. I was asleep.'

He sensed her relief as she heard the lie.

'All right, settle down now then.' She bent and kissed him goodnight. Her face felt hot and fevered. He put his arms round her and gave her a hug.

'Love you Rufus,' she said, pulling the duvet up over his shoulders. Then she turned away sadly and went out, closing the door behind her. The Nubbler came back to his position close to Rufus, and sat on the floor.

'I wish I could help her,' Rufus said.

'Well, there're things you can do,' the Nubbler said confidently.

'Are there? What?'

'Well, I'll show you as we go along.'

'I didn't do my homework.'

'No, I know. Don't worry. People can't do homework when they're scared. I'll come with you. It'll be all right.'

'*You'll* come with me? To *school*?'

'Yes.'

'They'll see you. They'll catch you.'

'No, they won't. They won't be able to see me. It's up to me, you see, Rufus. I can choose. There's only one person who knows I'm here.'

'What, *me*?' breathed Rufus.

'Yes, Rufus. Just you.'

CHAPTER TWO

In the morning the Nubbler had gone. Rufus looked anxiously round the room but nothing was different. He lay back in bed thinking. So had it just been a dream? He'd never had a dream that seemed so real. He could see the Nubbler quite clearly in his mind, the peering shortsighted eyes, the daft ears with little tufts on the ends. He could still feel the hard little hand on the back of his.

The Nubbler had said he would help him along, and by some means he knew what went on inside the house, the terrible arguments, the fear. Yet he had disappeared. Rufus felt an acute sense of loss. He suddenly remembered about his homework and his heart sank down to rock bottom.

'Rufus? Are you getting up?' His mother leant round the door in her dressing-gown. 'Come on, we're running a bit late.'

'Is Dad here?' he asked.

His mother paused. 'No. He's gone to work. He went early.'

Rufus looked at her face and felt a sense of dread fingering his stomach. She was lying. His dad hadn't come back at all. He had driven off enraged in the middle of the night, and he hadn't come home. He might never come home. He could have had an accident and be lying in his red car with nobody to help him. The Nubbler had gone as well. It had just been some kind of trick. There was no friend, no magic friend to help him. The idea was laughable. Here in this house with the anger and the shouting he was on his own just as he had always been.

Rufus got dressed, ate a breakfast he didn't want and set off for school.

CHAPTER THREE

Mr Croome normally taught Form 3 but he had hurt his back and, mad with frustration, was lying flat on a board at home.

At short notice Mr Carmichael, Head of the English Department, had been asked to stand in. Now he was in the classroom waiting for Form 3 to arrive, ready to teach this group for the first time and to start the business of getting to know those he had not yet met. He sat at the table in front of the class and heard the clamour as they approached.

Form 3 barged noisily into their form room, saw him and were immediately subdued. They were filled with a mixture of hope and trepidation. A new form teacher half-way through term was an interesting development, but a development which needed to be treated with caution. A third-rate form teacher could make life a misery. On the other hand, with a good one, life at school could be considerably enhanced. You could get to like a good one. The crowd of ten-year-old children, in an orderly fashion seldom seen, took their seats and sat weighing up Mr Carmichael. He looked very fit. He was a good-looking man and many girls in the school liked him a lot.

He waited, looking them over with his dark eyes. He did not smile.

Rufus sat down next to his best friend Eddie and waited in grim suspense for the moment when the homework was collected. He was scared and he watched the teacher without any hope of being saved. He did not have to wait long.

'Good morning, Form 3,' began Mr Carmichael in a strong, clear voice. 'For those of you in any doubt, I am Mr Carmichael, and I am in charge of the English Department.'

'Morning Mr Carmichael,' mumbled Form 3 self-consciously.

'I believe you were given homework to be handed in this morning?'

Rufus's heart lurched. This was it.

'Yes sir! Here sir!' volunteered Ian Watson who was keen about everything. He sat in a front desk and brandished his book noisily.

'Very well. Has everyone brought their homework?'

In a small wretched voice Rufus said, 'No sir.'

'And what is your name?'

'Clark sir, Rufus Clark.'

'And why haven't you brought it, Clark?'

'I forgot, sir,' Rufus lied. Ian Watson screwed round to get a better look at Rufus's misery.

'I see. Did anyone else forget?'

Rufus's eyes flicked round the classroom. No one murmured. Malcolm Keen, a big boy and a bully, watched steadily and hid the curious excitement he felt. Sarah Day liked Rufus and felt sorry for him. Each of them was agog to see what action the new teacher would take against a wrongdoer.

'See me at break, Clark.'

11

'Sir,' Rufus mumbled.

Mr Carmichael went on with the lesson. Rufus sat numbly, not listening to any of it, lost in his own thoughts. He thought about his dad, about where he might be. He thought about his mum and whether she was still at home. He thought about having started off on the wrong foot with this new teacher. He thought about the Nubbler.

Mr Carmichael set about getting to know his new class. He asked them their names and what subjects they liked best. He asked about any trips, any days out the school had arranged for them, what they'd enjoyed. He asked all these questions, listened carefully to the answers, and all the time was watching Rufus Clark. He took in the pallor of the boy's skin, the dark circles under the eyes, his lost, haunted look. Mr Carmichael had no doubt that something was wrong, very seriously wrong.

The bell went for break.

'Good luck, Rufus,' said Eddie in a stage whisper as he got up to file out with the others. Rufus nodded. Everyone left. Mr Carmichael stood up, walked across and closed the blue painted door. He returned to his desk and sat down.

'Come here, Rufus,' he said.

Rufus got to his feet and walked to the front. He was scared and tensed up, the waiting had lasted for ever. He stood looking down at the floor.

'Well, look up.'

Rufus looked up into Mr Carmichael's calm face. His voice was quite friendly.

'Now. How did you come to forget your homework?'

Rufus shrugged. Automatically he said, 'Don't know, sir.'

'You don't know.'

'No sir.'

12

'I see. But you wrote the essay?'

'Yes sir,' Rufus replied without thinking, and then realised with a jolt what he'd said.

'On what subject?'

Mr Carmichael waited.

'What was the subject of the essay?'

Rufus looked down at the floor, trapped.

Softly, into the agonised silence floated the suggestion of a pine-tree smell. Small hard fingers gently closed over Rufus's clammy hand. He could see nothing but his heart leapt up for joy. It was the Nubbler! The Nubbler! He was here!

In his back Rufus felt a small encouraging push.

He looked up and faced the teacher. 'I didn't do it,' he said, 'I'm sorry.'

Incredibly he thought he saw an amused light dancing in the eyes of Mr Carmichael, but he must have been mistaken.

'I see. Thank you. Why not?'

'Don't know, sir.'

'You don't know.'

'No sir.'

'Can you do it tonight?'

'Sir.'

Then Mr Carmichael asked a startlingly direct question.

'Is it easy for you to work at home, Rufus?'

'Yes sir,' replied Rufus automatically.

Mr Carmichael looked at the boy intently for a moment and then relaxed, leaning back in his chair. 'Good. That's it then. Off you go or you'll miss break.'

In Rufus's chest the great, pricked balloon of fear gently deflated, folding in upon itself. It was all over. Nothing terrible had happened.

Awash with relief he floated out of the classroom. The Nubbler, completely invisible, floated out close behind him.

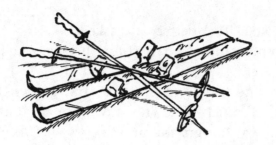

CHAPTER FOUR

Dad came home that evening at the normal time. Mum was cooking the tea and Rufus was sitting up to the kitchen table doing his homework. Mum said hello to him in a false, bright voice and Dad grunted sulkily back to her. Tea was terrible. Mum kept up this act that everything was fine and friendly, chatting gaily to Rufus. It was so stupid, while his dad sat there with a face like thunder. She must think Rufus was blind. As if he couldn't feel that something was wrong! He couldn't wait for tea to be over so he could go up to his room, shut his door, shut them out.

Mum finished cooking the tea and placed the plates before them. Rufus looked down at the brightly coloured carrots and the brown splodge of gravy. There was the sort of silence you could cut with a knife. His heart was beating fast. This was all going to blow up, any minute now.

'No thanks,' said Dad, glancing dismissively at his plate.

Mum stared at him, outraged.

'Well, thanks for letting me cook it!' she spat.

'You're welcome!' Dad said cleverly.

Something snapped in Mum. She marched over, snatched up his plate of bright food, yanked open the cupboard under

15

the sink and whacked the whole thing into the bin, plate and all.

Dad smirked. 'Feel better?' he asked.

Mum spun round to face him, her face red, her eyes glittering.

Rufus, in one wide sweep of his arm, gathered in all his homework. He ducked down away from the table, leaving the food he was hungry for, and ran away. Dropped pencils tinkled behind him. He barged up the stairs to his room and sat on the bed shaking with fear, waiting for the storm to break downstairs.

Suddenly the room filled with the fresh woody smell and the Nubbler was beside him, looking at him intently.

'You have a lie down, Rufus,' he said.

'Lie down? What do I want to *lie down* for?' Rufus snapped, 'There's going to be an almighty row down there! Mum might leave home!'

'No.' The Nubbler shook his head confidently. 'No, she won't, Rufus. You can forget that. She loves you, she'll never go. You lie down. It's not very good here. I'm going to take you somewhere. We'll come back when it's all over.'

'What? Where're you going to take me?'

'You'll see. Somewhere nice. Lie down and close your eyes. Get under the covers. Get warm.'

Rufus took off his big black shoes and climbed under the duvet still wearing his school clothes. The Nubbler sat on the floor beside the bed. Downstairs there were angry shouts and the scrape of a chair being thrust back from the table.

'Keep your eyes closed, Rufus. We're going away now. And don't be frightened. Remember, you can do it. You've learned how to do it.' The Nubbler's hand closed tightly over his.

The first thing Rufus felt was the cold. Icy cold air rushed at his face. The second thing he noticed was the sound, a high-pitched slicing, singing sound. He was moving fast through snow and trees, his weight thrown forward against the hard fronts of big grey boots.

Rufus was on skis. He had never skied before but he was skiing now. He zoomed down a wide snowy path through Christmas trees bent and burdened with snow. His heart felt light and he was thrilled, thrilled beyond anything he had felt before. He just suddenly knew how to do it, he put his weight on the lower leg and turned, did it again and turned back, zigzagging smoothly down the endless snowy slope.

He was warm and padded up in a bright coat. He had on padded blue trousers, gloves, hat and goggles. He was surrounded by people he knew to be his friends. Eddie was skiing beside him. Eddie couldn't ski either, not really, but here he was, soaring along, his face a mask of excitement and joy.

There was a man in front, an adult. He was looking round, checking them, making sure they were all right. It was hard to see the adult's face, but Rufus had the feeling he knew him, knew him and liked him a lot.

On the other side of Rufus was a different boy, one he had not seen before. He knew he was Chinese and he knew his name was Anthony but he didn't know how he knew. They skied on down the long, long slope. Cascades of snow slid from trees as they flashed past, and the freed branches sprang up lightly. They were laughing, overjoyed, their weight thrown forward, knees bent, poles in their hands.

They passed close to a great steel structure like a pylon. It was part of a ski-lift. From up on the suspended seats people

17

called down to them, their skis dangling into space. Rufus, Eddie and Anthony shouted and whooped back.

At last the slope began to level out and the man in front called back to them. A big foreign-looking chalet came into view and they turned towards it, slowing down. There was a table laden with cheeses and sticks of french bread. There were bowls of soup and tomatoes and hot flaky croissants with a thick seam of chocolate all through.

Laughing and exhausted and happier than ever before Rufus stopped, stepped on the bindings of his skis to release them, and clumped in big boots with Eddie and Anthony towards the table, to sit down for the meal of a lifetime.

When the argument between his parents finally ended, they looked around, realised that Rufus had fled, and went to his room to find him. They edged in guiltily and saw that their son was asleep under his duvet. He'd had nothing to eat. His big black shoes were askew on the floor, and he was fully dressed in school clothes.

CHAPTER FIVE

At school the bell rang to mark the end of break and the wide school corridors filled with roaring rivers of children. Waves of them surged in opposite directions and they grappled through each other amid the peculiar smell of school itself, hot cross-country bodies, wet leather shoes, pungent school dinners. Relieved and gasping, Form 3 cut away from the main stream and gushed into their classroom. The playground footballers collapsed red-faced and panting into their chairs. Mr Carmichael studied them. He thought Rufus Clark looked healthier.

'Good morning,' Mr Carmichael began. 'Who has heard of UNICEF?'

'Me! Me sir!' Ian Watson flapped a thin arm.

'You, Watson,' invited Mr Carmichael.

'It's a children's charity, sir! It looks after children!'

'You're right, Watson, well done. It looks after children. Over the next month the school is planning to raise money for UNICEF. Can you suggest a way to go about it? Anyone?'

'Sponsored swim, sir!' Ian Watson volunteered.

'Sponsored walk,' said Sarah Day.

'Do face painting,' offered Jude Davey and blushed. She

was Sarah's best friend. She had a fervent crush on Mr Carmichael and thought about him all the time.

'Sponsored bike ride!' shouted Eddie.

Mr Carmichael studied them all. Rufus thought what a nice face he had. Often, like now, he could look dead serious, but in his eyes there was this light which made you think he was trying not to laugh.

'Thank you,' he said, 'for your suggestions, all of which we could certainly do. I would however, like you to consider an alternative. A Home Clothes Day. Anyone know what it is?'

'You wear home clothes, sir!' Ian Watson again.

'Indeed. You wear home clothes. You leave your uniform at home and ... wear anything you like.'

A gasp of joy ran through Form 3. Anything they liked! They turned to each other excitedly, loudly suggesting wild and outlandish outfits, laughing, outdoing each other. Sarah and Jude turned to the girls behind, offering outrageous dares.

'But!' boomed Mr Carmichael. An expectant hush fell on the room. 'But ... you will have to PAY!'

The expected groan was loud and protracted.

'How much? How much sir?'

'Whatever you can genuinely afford. Everyone's circumstances are different. Bring what you can and in return, I expect to be POLE-AXED by your ELEGANCE as you come into school NEXT FRIDAY. I'll give out a communication for your parents at the end of the lesson. A what, Keen?'

'A communication, sir!' said Malcolm Keen, who had been talking.

'Correct. Please give it to your parents, don't place it in your desk, your pocket or your sports bag and then remember

20

it six months later. Let us all try to do this well, to help other people.'

'Are you going to dress up, sir?' Rachel asked boldly from the back.

'Certainly not, Rachel,' Mr Carmichael replied with a grin, 'I maintain my standards at all times.' This was greeted by good-natured jeers, and Jude thought to herself that yes, it was true, he did always look nice.

This was something good, something different. Form 3 were in an enthusiastic mood.

'Before we go on,' Mr Carmichael interrupted the excited murmuring, 'there is one more thing. We have a new boy joining our class on Monday and I ask you to be especially considerate. It's hard for anyone to join a new school, particularly in the middle of term. He is Chinese. His family has recently moved here from Hong Kong, so you can imagine that he is having to contend with a great deal of change. A new country, with new customs, a different climate, and a different language. I hope you will do your best to help him settle in.'

There was much interested nodding. Only Rufus was motionless.

'What's his name, sir?' asked Sarah Day.

Rufus did not need to listen to the reply. He knew the name of the Chinese boy. The Nubbler had shown him. It was Anthony.

'Anthony,' replied Mr Carmichael clearly. 'His name is Anthony Wan.'

Rufus sat stock still and felt the prickle run up his back. It ran up his spine, over the back of his neck and faded away into his hair.

CHAPTER SIX

The next day Mum came in from work. She unloaded the shopping into the fridge, made herself a cup of coffee and sat down at the kitchen table.

She worked part-time in a fabric shop in town. She enjoyed dressmaking herself and was good at helping people to choose patterns, materials, tapes to gather up curtains, buttons, buckles and a thousand other things. She liked her job and Leila, the friend she worked with. Being busy in the different environment of the shop allowed her to forget how unhappy she often was at home.

Mr Carmichael's letter from school was on the table. She reread it, smiling at the piece about wearing home clothes, knowing exactly which outfit Rufus would choose.

Her brother Allan lived in Queensland, Australia. He worked hard in the building trade, his wife Tessa worked at one of the airports and they had modestly prospered. They came back from time to time. Allan was a big man with a port-wine birthmark on his jaw. He was terrific with children and Rufus idolised him. He called Rufus 'Roof' and sent his nephew bizarre gifts including a hideous T-shirt and baseball cap which was supposed to be a crocodile catcher's outfit.

Both the T-shirt and hat had great teeth marks in them, and were all soaked and spattered with fake blood. A great bloody bite had been removed from the peak of the cap. Rufus valued these two items of clothing above all others.

She would search them out and wash them for him. Mum smiled and put the letter aside. Turning to the newspaper on the table, she leafed through it and stopped at the entertainments page, running her finger down the list.

There were dances but Dad didn't dance. At least he didn't dance with her. She looked down the list of films at the local cinema and saw a new Oscar-winner with her favourite actor. Even in the little box showing the film title the Oscars had been depicted, standing up like bottles. She considered seeing it on one of her free afternoons. Perhaps Leila would like to go with her.

She brightened up, finished her coffee, looked at her watch and started to make the dough for a pizza.

CHAPTER SEVEN

'Form 3, I would like you to meet Anthony Wan, who joins us today. Good morning Anthony, we're pleased to have you with us.' Mr Carmichael gave him a warm smile.

'Fang you sir,' replied Anthony in a Chinese voice.

Malcolm Keen laughed. He caught a laser-like look of warning from Mr Carmichael, but it was too late, Anthony had heard. His dark, almond eyes were filled with uncertainty. He was afraid of this new school in a strange, cold country and yearned for his familiar home in Hong Kong.

Uncomfortable in the stiff new uniform, in coarse grey trousers which prickled and irritated his legs, he longed for the soft, washed-out shorts and open-necked shirt he had worn to school at home. He ached for the lights on the mountainous skyline, the furious water traffic on the harbour, the familiar smells and sounds of his beloved home on the other side of the world. He opened his brand-new exercise book and stared down at the blank page in despair.

When the bell went for lunch he nearly jumped out of his skin. There was an instant eruption of noise and action. Desk lids were yanked up, books thudded inside and all around him people sat electrified, waiting.

'Please hand in your work as you leave,' said Mr Carmichael.

'I feel sick, sir!' said Ian Watson suddenly in a small panic-stricken voice.

Mr Carmichael flashed a look at him, saw the stretched greenish skin on his face, cursed himself for being so concerned with Anthony that he had failed to notice Ian was ill.

'Oh, right Ian. Rufus? Take Ian to the cloakroom, quickly. Then see him to the sickroom. Go now.'

Rufus and Ian bundled out of the door, followed after a brief pause by all the others. Mr Carmichael turned back to the work on his desk, then suddenly realised that in attending to Ian he had forgotten to appoint a boy to show Anthony Wan the dining-hall. He gathered up the books, intending to follow quickly to make sure that Anthony was all right.

This plan was foiled by a discreet tap on the door which opened to reveal the school secretary, Mrs Shaw, with a clipboard under her arm. Her head was tilted, birdlike, to one side. She wondered if he could pop into her office for a moment on his way to lunch. Could he be so kind?

In the queue outside the dining-hall the noise was extraordinary as the entire school waited for the blue doors to open. Through the opaque glass they could make out figures rushing up and down the tables, placing last-minute jugs and plastic tumblers. Anthony stood in the thick of the crowd, utterly alone. Eddie tried to catch his eye to smile, but Anthony was too afraid to look up. Malcolm Keen spotted him. Something about the boy's cowed appearance gave him

25

a sharp flicker of excitement and he sauntered over. Anthony shot him a wary glance as he approached.

Malcolm Keen came close, too close. He towered over the new boy and hemmed him in. Anthony could feel the heat and menace coming off him.

'Hello,' he slowly breathed. 'Hello. Me old chop suey.'

There was a shout of laughter from Malcolm's cronies. Eddie took a step towards Anthony to try to help him, but Anthony turned, his face filled with panic, and fled back the way he had come.

'You shouldn't've done that! You shouldn't have said that to him!' shouted Eddie. His voice was lost as the blue doors opened and the tidal wave of children swept in, ravenous, desperate.

Rufus just managed to get Ian to the cloakroom before he was sick. He stood outside the cubicle listening to the unwelcome sounds of Ian retching, gasping and spitting in disgust. 'Don't let any of the smell reach me,' Rufus silently prayed.

'You OK, Ian?' he asked, controlling his revulsion.

'No,' came a small wretched voice.

'You OK to get to the sickroom? Can you make it that far?'

'Dunno. Wait a minute. You'll have to wait a minute.'

There was more coughing and spitting and the sound of the lavatory being flushed. Then Ian, ashen-faced and with watering eyes, appeared at the door like a wraith.

'Come on, Ian,' said Rufus kindly, 'you can lie down up there.'

Rufus escorted Ian to the sickroom and left him there with the nurse. Then he walked back down the stairs and along the empty, silent corridors towards the dining-hall. His footsteps rang out. Everyone was at lunch. He supposed all the best food would have gone. It didn't matter. Listening at such close range to Ian being sick had done nothing for his appetite.

He was passing their form room when he felt the Nubbler's hand stop him. It pushed him in the chest.

'What?' he whispered. 'What's wrong?'

Now the little hand pushed him from the side, steering him towards the door of the classroom.

'In here?' asked Rufus in a tiny whisper.

Another push.

Rufus opened the door and walked into the classroom. He stopped, shocked. Anthony Wan was alone in the room. He was doubled up in his chair, his fist stuffed in his mouth, tears streaming down his face. When he looked up, his haunted expression did something to Rufus. It made him angry. Angry and ashamed. He thought of Mr Carmichael asking them to help the new boy settle in. He thought of Malcolm Keen smirking and sniggering when Anthony spoke, and he guessed the rest. He walked over and said in a friendly voice:

'Come on Anthony, it's all right. You come to lunch with me and Eddie, we'll make sure you're OK. You can stay with us. Have you got a handkerchief?'

Anthony took out a large, clean, neatly folded handkerchief and mopped his face.

'Fang you,' he said, 'fang you vey much.'

Mr Carmichael strode quickly from Mrs Shaw's depressing office to the dining-hall. Once inside he scanned the rows of bobbing heads for Anthony Wan. He was not there. He frowned as he checked again. Suddenly the door on the opposite side of the hall opened and Rufus Clark ushered

Anthony in. It was clear, even from this distance, that Anthony had been in tears. He watched as the two boys threaded their way along the tables and sat down next to Eddie. Mr Carmichael looked around for Malcolm Keen, found him and caught his eye in a long expressionless look.

CHAPTER EIGHT

Dad was a salesman but he hated it. He worked for a company called Elegance Fitted Bedrooms. They made wardrobes, dressing-tables, chests of drawers, whatever the client wanted. It was Dad's job to go out to people's homes and persuade them to buy from Elegance rather than anyone else. He had big cumbersome books to show the client. These were filled with special graph paper on which he stuck little pictures of the furniture to show people what their new bedroom was supposed to look like when it was finished.

Dad did not enjoy the work. He hated fiddling around with the little pictures, and he also knew that the quality of the furniture was poor and that it wouldn't last. Now he sat in the kitchen of a Mr and Mrs Nelson, giving them the well-practised sales patter.

'These are made in our own workshops, by craftsmen,' he said, as he had been taught to say.

Craftsmen. That was a laugh. It was great ham-fisted Tiger Mullins who threw the stuff together. Dad pictured him in his brown overall, standing ape-like in the woodshavings on the workshop floor. Some craftsman. Tiger couldn't care less.

Dad continued with the rehearsed sales patter: 'Not only

that, but the furniture you choose will be fitted in your own home with a minimum of fuss, probably inside *two days*.'

'Two days!' mousy Mrs Nelson fluttered excitedly. She was sick of her old, cluttered bedroom. 'That's good, isn't it, Maurice?'

'Oh, um, yes,' replied Maurice in what he hoped was a forthright, head-of-the-household sort of way, 'jolly good.'

'How much would it cost then, with the ornament shelves?' ventured Mrs Nelson. She had the bit between her teeth now. She could see herself, young and gorgeous as she had never been, seated at the Hollywood-style dressing-table in a glamorous robe. She imagined herself brushing out her long burnished hair as Maurice watched, swamped by the lavish hangings of the four poster bed.

Dad tapped the figures into his calculator. 'Give you a bit of discount ...' he said confidingly, in the way he had been shown on the selling courses. Mrs Nelson fluttered again. He tapped the total button with a flourish and leant back in the chair, satisfied.

'Two thousand five hundred pounds,' he pronounced, '*and* you qualify for interest-free credit.'

He knew Mrs Nelson would agree, whatever he said. He had been shown how to wind people up, he knew the technique.

'Oh *yes* Maurice, let's have it!' she twittered, spending the poor old fool's money. 'We've never had anything nice for ourselves.'

Maurice looked at her uncertainly. Dad stared at him with another of his well-rehearsed looks. This one was of open admiration that any man could be so generous to his wife. Maurice was trapped.

'Well, all right then, yes, we'll have it!' he declared and in so doing took on a debt he could not afford. Maurice had no idea that his entrapment had been carefully mapped out, word for word, stage by stage, by men schooled in the dubious art of selling.

Dad filled in the forms with them, shook hands and left. As he loaded the big books back into the car the genial smile faded and disappeared from his face. He started the car and drove off.

The whole thing left a bitter taste in his mouth. He saw Maurice, confused, not wanting to lose face by refusing to order. He saw Tiger Mullins assembling their shoddy bits of furniture. They would expect so much and get so little. The drawers would stick, the cheap gilt handles would come off and Mrs Nelson's Hollywood-style mirror would swing uselessly in its trashy fittings. All their complaints, their feeble telephone calls and ill-composed letters would be received by the company, and be totally ignored.

Dad was on commission, which meant the more he sold, the more he earned. Well, it was a lousy job, but at least he would now have a bit of extra cash. As he drove along he thought of his home and his rotten marriage and of his poor son Rufus stuck in the middle.

A clipboard was lying on the worn upholstery of the passenger seat. Dad glanced at it for the address of the next clients and his spirits sank further. It was so many miles away. His neck and shoulders were already beginning to ache as he steered the company car round the roundabout, down the slip road and out on to the greasy motorway.

He let himself think about his old job, and felt an unbearable, piercing pain. Once, in what seemed like another life, he had worked for a garden centre. It had been owned by the same family for years. The company did a lot

31

of landscape gardening. Dad used to drive a white pick-up truck loaded with young trees, shrubs, sacks of compost and tightly coiled rolls of turf. He and his mate Arch would turn up at some new house where the garden was just a sea of builder's rubble, and set to work to transform it.

With a digger they scraped away the rubbish and broken bricks, and stabbed the hard compacted soil deep down to let in air and life. He and Arch dug out ponds and laid cable for fountains and pumps. They built patios and winding paths, levelling the paving slabs with taps to the corners.

Tipper trucks came to heap on fine, sieved topsoil, and in rich, foody compost they planted trees, shrubs, borders. Staggering under the weight, they unrolled green carpets of turf, and placed new seats on new lawns, under new trees, by new pools.

Dad felt a desolate sense of loss and shook his head in disbelief. He had loved that job so much, and now he had to settle for this. This job conning people. This job of trickery and disappointment.

That first job had been about building up, about creating something new and worthwhile. Years afterwards, he still drove past gardens which he and Arch had planted, saw people sitting out under trees grown big, with kids playing and little bikes on the lawns. It was agony to think about it, even now.

A supermarket had bought the land. The garden centre was near a busy road leading out of town, and a supermarket bought the site. The family who owned the garden centre were sad to see their longstanding business close, but they were offered an enormous sum of money. They chose security, comfort and freedom from money worries. Who could blame them for that? It was what everybody dreamed about. Dad didn't blame them.

But there had been something else. Somebody else. The family had a daughter called Eunice, about the same age as Dad. She had been like him, she loved the place and worked there every day to learn the business.

A strange sad smile came over Dad's face while he pictured her as she was then, chatting to customers at the till, spraying young plants in the big greenhouses, feeding and stroking rabbits in the pet section.

He'd longed to ask her out, but he'd been young and flustered because she was the daughter of the owner, from a family with money, and he had nothing, nothing at all.

Well, the garden centre disappeared under a supermarket and the employees scattered over a wide area. As time passed they took up new lives. Arch scraped a living as a painter and decorator. Dad met and married Mum, Rufus was born and suddenly he had a twenty-five year mortgage. Every month there was a bill.

He had taken the job with Elegance Fitted Bedrooms as a stopgap, something to tide him over until he found some-thing he enjoyed. Well, nothing had turned up. He applied for jobs like his old one on the rare occasions they were advertised, but now his age was beginning to count against him and he had no degree.

He began to feel trapped. At home he and Mum started to argue and bicker as slowly even the friendship drained out of their marriage.

Anyway, something had happened, something weird. One day the address on the clipboard turned out to be Eunice's.

He drove out to this white house with greenhouses and

who should come to the door but Eunice. He was thunder-struck, they both were. Suddenly it was like they'd never been apart and it came to Dad with enormous force and certainty that he had quite simply married the wrong person. He should have married Eunice. He loved her before and he loved her now, and she felt just the same. Yet he loved his son Rufus as well, and did not want to hurt Mum.

So, turning this way and that, Dad struggled in his quagmire of indecision. From Monday to Friday he drove his red car up and down the endless motorways like a dead-eyed tiger pacing the bars of a cage.

He felt himself getting older, felt the years haring past as he worked at a job he loathed to pay for a life which wasn't the life he wanted. He felt used, trapped, desperate; and at home in ghastly scenes this uncontainable anger exploded at Mum, who didn't deserve it.

He crept like a thief to visit Eunice, stood quietly in her big greenhouse and dreamed of another life where all the people who deserved to be happy could be happy, where there were no big books, no clipboard, and no catastrophic making of wrong decisions.

CHAPTER NINE

With Dad away there was nothing to frighten Rufus in the house. On Thursday night he had his tea with Mum. He told her what he was going to wear to school for Home Clothes Day the following morning. Mum feigned horror but she had already gathered the clothes up. In the airing cupboard they were washed and waiting. Everything was ready for tomorrow, the crocodile top and hat, the threadbare jeans, the favourite orange socks.

'You'll look *awful!*' she scolded, laughing. 'Give me my purse while I think of it.' She gave him two pounds for the UNICEF collection. Together they ate rice pudding at the kitchen table. Dad's place was empty and unlaid.

'What time's Dad coming home, Mum?' asked Rufus.

'Tomorrow. He'll be back tomorrow afternoon. He's away tonight, up north.' She said it too fast and Rufus didn't believe his dad was up north.

In the morning Rufus dressed with the utmost slowness, savouring the unique experience of putting on his cherished crocodile catcher outfit on a *school* morning. He stared with satisfaction at the orange socks: how they clashed with the bloody spatters on the top and hat. His white skin glistened behind the denim-stranded holes in the knees of his jeans. He adjusted the angle of the hat, and sprang downstairs to breakfast and the satisfyingly outraged reaction of his mum.

He set off to school clutching the two pounds, filled with respect for Mr Carmichael and his truly brilliant idea of the Home Clothes Day.

CHAPTER TEN

From his study on the first floor, the Headmaster gazed down upon the arriving pupils with mounting horror. They looked like a column of refugees fleeing some unspeakable war, and he wondered again how he had let Mr Carmichael talk him into it.

A forest of legs in frayed old jeans sauntered towards the main entrance. In swaggered T-shirts, sweatshirts, drop-dead leather jackets all with studs, tassels, images of popstars, vampires or dubious slogans. Back-to-front baseball caps and a wild assortment of other hats topped off the picture. The overall effect was of a travelling rummage sale. It was desperately hard to tell girls from boys and the Headmaster, unnerved, shook his head in a no-good-will-come-of-this sort of way.

There was much excitement in the packed corridors downstairs, and a rising wall of noise. Each arriving outfit was evaluated with gasps of admiration or harsh jeers. Rufus in the crocodile ensemble had a huge advantage, in that it had come from Australia and no one else had anything like it. His outfit made the popstar tops look tame. Rufus was proud and tugged the bitten hat down over one eye to look cool.

Ian Watson wore jeans, but they were neatly pressed with a knife-sharp crease down the front which made them nearly as bad as uniform. Malcolm Keen looked thuggish in a blackish sweatshirt and unsavoury jogging bottoms. The twins Nick and Sam Diamond had brought flashing bow ties for a laugh but now were too embarrassed to put them on.

There was one person they all wanted to see and that was Eddie. His dad worked a lot in the States and the word was that he had brought back something sensational for Eddie to wear.

They did not have to wait long. Suddenly, quietly, Eddie emerged from the cloakroom and a hush fell on them all. They were dumbstruck. They had known it was going to be good of course, but this was something else.

Eddie wore what looked like a red crash helmet. It was very streamlined with ventilation slits along the sides. Had it only been a crash helmet it would have been impressive, but it was considerably more. It was a radio and CD player. It fitted right over his head and ears with an aerial sticking out of the top and controls along the front. It looked fantastic, incredibly cool.

Everyone gathered round, fingering it respectfully. They pleaded in imploring voices to be allowed to try it on. Eddie listened indulgently to their petitions like a king in his crown. Secure, assured, he glanced from one to the other.

Then the steel bar on the door rattled loudly as it was seized. The door swung open and silence fell. In the entrance stood Anthony Wan. Everyone turned to look at him. They looked him up and down in disbelief. Rufus's heart sank, sank right down into his boots.

Anthony was wearing a three-piece suit. He just stood there in the doorway in a three-piece business suit with a waist-coat. His parents, not really understanding the idea, had insisted that he dress in the formal style of his own country. Draped across the front of the waistcoat was a gold watch and chain. He stood completely still. Only his brown eyes ranged over the jeans, the tops, the leather jackets of the others.

'Well, well, well.' Malcolm Keen swaggered to the front, his hands thrust in his pockets, his eyes cruel and bright. 'If it ain't the bank manager ...'

There were a few nervous titters. Malcolm looked Anthony up and down, lingering on the big watch. 'I wonder,' he asked in a mocking voice, 'I wonder if you could tell us the time?'

There was unpleasant laughter. Rufus couldn't stand the look on Anthony's face, couldn't bear to see his pitiful isolation as the bully closed in. He knew he was bound to get pasted by Malcolm, who was much bigger than he, but he just couldn't stand there and look on. The funny thing was, the Nubbler didn't push him. He knew the Nubbler was beside him, as always, but no push came. It was as if the Nubbler was letting him decide for himself.

'Pack it up, Malcolm,' Rufus said.

Malcolm turned to him. 'What?' he said in a low voice.

'I said pack it up. This is Home Clothes Day. We've all worn what we'd put on at home and just because Anthony comes from a different place doesn't mean we all have to stand round laughing. Grow up.'

To Rufus's amazement, there was a murmur of agreement.

'Yeah, leave him alone,' said Nick Diamond bravely.

'I think you look very smart, Anthony,' said Sarah Day, going a bit over the top.

'So do I,' said Jude.

Eddie got it right. 'Come on Anthony,' he said, 'don't stand there in the door. Do you want to try my hat?'

Rufus stood back and watched in amazement. The others surged forward, ushering Anthony to the front to be equipped with the magnificent hat. Malcolm Keen was left standing alone. The swagger went out of his stance and he seemed to sag. He met Rufus's eyes and held them malevolently. He said nothing. All he did was to level a finger at Rufus and point. He held it for a second, then turned and walked away. Rufus had no doubt that it meant trouble.

Nevertheless the extraordinary thing was that he, Rufus, had turned the situation round. He had never done that before, never considered it. He had spoken up and, unexpectedly, others had agreed with him.

He turned and looked at them, then looked at Anthony. The handsome red radio hat was jammed well down on his head and his fingers were twiddling madly with the buttons on the front. People reached out to touch the glossy, ruby red plastic. They stroked it and ran the whippy silver aerial through their fingers. Anthony stood in their midst smiling, deafened by the roaring music, his gold watch tucked securely into his waistcoat pocket.

Rufus, watching, put his arm out a little way. Had anyone else noticed they might have thought it an uncomfortable position, stuck there in mid air. But it wasn't at all. His arm was firmly round the shoulders of the Nubbler.

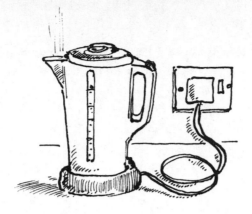

CHAPTER ELEVEN

On Friday afternoon Dad pulled into the drive. He yanked on the handbrake, switched off the ignition and slumped wearily back in his seat. Comforting stillness settled around him after the grinding journey. The Friday afternoon roads had been choked with traffic. The engine ticked as it cooled. He was home. Home at last.

After a while he stirred, unhooked his jacket, grasped the big books. He'd have a cup of tea with Mum, then a long bath. Try and get things on more of an even keel for Rufus's sake. Weighed down by the big books he walked to the front door and found it locked against him. He pushed at it a couple of times aggressively, then fumbled for his keys and let himself in.

The place was cold and silent. No voice called to him. It was neat, tidy and deserted. He put down the books and walked through to the kitchen. She wouldn't be at work, she never worked on Friday afternoons. So where was she? There was no note, nothing.

He put the kettle on, switched on the immersion heater for his bath, and sat down at the table. Great. Some homecoming after the two days he'd had. The place was as quiet as the grave. His irritation rose as he waited and wondered.

CHAPTER TWELVE

In their form room Mr Carmichael was reading to them from something funny. They were all in a good mood. At the end he closed the book and walked round to the front of his table. He eyed them all.

'Today has been Home Clothes Day and you have all looked very ... interesting,' he said in a controlled way. They laughed. 'I hope you've found it an enjoyable experience?'

They all nodded enthusiastically. He noticed with relief that Anthony, in the inappropriate suit, nodded as eagerly as the rest.

'Good. I'm also pleased to tell you that the participating forms have raised just over £140, which is a good result by any standard. This was an idea which hadn't been tried in the school before and you've made it a resounding success. Well done everyone.'

Rufus said, 'It was brilliant, sir. When can we do it again?'

Mr Carmichael nodded and smiled. 'Thank you, Rufus. I think the memory of this one may last us for a little while.'

More laughter. Jude beamed at him from between two alarming yellow earrings.

'However, I do have another idea. I would be glad to know what you think of it.'

Nick Diamond said, 'What sir? What is it?'

In the short silence before Mr Carmichael answered, Rufus felt the prickle form. It travelled slowly up his back. He felt the hairs at the nape of his neck stand right up as Mr Carmichael replied.

'A skiing holiday, Nick. A skiing trip, to France.'

CHAPTER THIRTEEN

Rufus walked home from school feeling happy. He was still wearing the crocodile catcher's outfit as he sauntered up the road. Leaves had started to come off the trees now and long drifts of them gathered in the angles between pavement and wall. He kicked them up a bit and shied at them with his sports bag. They were soggy underneath and smeared his orange socks.

It just suddenly occurred to him that he was going home through the housing estate feeling happy. So very often he had walked along here, dragging his feet, afraid to go home. The Nubbler had come and changed all that.

Rufus thought about Mr Carmichael, about how much he liked him. He thought about the way he, Rufus, had helped Anthony today when he was being picked on, and how good that had made him feel. He thought about his best friend Eddie and the hat. And he thought about the skiing trip, the amazing, scary, thrilling business of the skiing trip. Well, he was going. If he had to wash cars and dig gardens for the money, if he had to *slave*, he was going skiing with Mr Carmichael to France.

He was rehearsing how he would ask Mum to let him go as

he turned into their close and saw his dad's red car parked in the drive. Mum's much older car was parked at the kerbside. In an instant Rufus felt that all was not well. He approached the house hesitantly, heard the shouting voices and felt all his cheerfulness drain away. Familiar icy fear seeped into him. He let himself silently into the house and sat down on the foot of the stairs, listening. His parents were in the kitchen.

'A film?' bawled his father. 'And who'd you go to see *a film* with?'

'Leila! I told you! I went with Leila!'

'Oh yes, sure!' sneered Dad, his voice dripping scorn.

'Yes I did, you can ask her! I wanted to see a film! I wanted to go out for once!'

'Yeah, and if I hadn't come home early I'd never have found out!'

'Found out?' Mum's voice was high and squealing. 'Found out what? There was nothing to find out!'

'Liar!' Dad said quietly, in contempt.

How they hated each other. They lived together in this house in flaring hatred. There was nothing Rufus could do, he was helpless. He loved them both, loved them with all his heart but he couldn't change a thing. They tore into each other with their vicious words and loathing looks and he had to sit on the sidelines terrified, watch the persecution of his mother, the brutal raging of his father, knowing that whatever it took to stop them and make things right was not available to a boy of ten.

Suddenly his father broke away, barged out through the sitting-room and made for the front door. His eyes had a white demented glitter. With a jolt he saw Rufus sitting on the stairs, and sagged with grief.

'Oh Rufus, not you!' he groaned through his gritted teeth. Shaking his head he wrenched open the front door, backed the car out like a madman and roared off. Driving like that he could kill somebody.

Rufus could hear his mother's racked dry sobs in the kitchen. He got up and walked in to her. She was standing curled over in the corner, one hand up to her face, her mouth in a terrible sobbing grin. Rufus went over to her, put his arms round her waist and laid his face awkwardly against her arm.

'Never mind, Mum,' he said.

She sobbed and turned to him, holding him tightly.

'Oh Rufus, have you heard all this?' she groaned.

He wasn't going to lie any more. 'Yes, I was on the stairs. I always hear everything. I could hear you from outside.'

'Your dad thinks I've got a boyfriend.'

'Yeah, I heard him. You haven't, have you?'

Mum shook her head. 'I just went with Leila to see a film.'

'You're not going to leave us, are you, Mum?' Rufus asked, dreading her answer.

His mum tightened her arms around him. Then she got down on one knee so she was level with him and he was staring straight into her poor wet face. She looked at him for a long time and when at last she spoke her voice had a queer edge he had not heard before. It was as if she had made a decision long overdue.

'Look Rufus, you're only ten. I hate having to talk to you about this. But Dad and I have had it. You can see that. We can't go on like this. *You* can't go on like this. But wherever I go Rufus, *you're* coming with me. There's no question of me leaving *you*. You're the best thing in the world and I love you millions.'

47

Rufus sensed that she was saying something big and dreadful, something of awesome importance.

'What about Dad?' he whispered.

'You'll see Dad. He loves you too. You'll see him.'

'But where will he be?'

'I don't know that, Rufus. But I think it's best now if your dad and I think about living apart. I'll make some enquiries but you and I, we may even be able to stay on in this house. And I won't shut you out any more. I'll tell you everything as soon as I know it myself. But listen, you and I, we'll be together, I'm not going *anywhere* without you. Do you understand that?'

Rufus was fighting to grasp what she meant.

'What, Dad'll go? You mean Dad'll go away somewhere?'

Mum took a huge deep breath.

'I expect so. Dad has had another ... friend for a long time now. Another lady. I expect he'll finish up there.' She saw the look of pain and confusion on his face and added in a rush: 'But you'll see Dad. He won't be far away. You'll see your dad as often as you want.' Mum faltered and went on, 'Dad and I, well, we don't love each other now, Rufus. We did once but ... well, not any more. But he loves *you*, he loves you just as much as I do.'

Rufus looked steadily into her puffy eyes. 'This is divorce, isn't it, Mum?' he asked.

Mum nodded. Tears suddenly filled her eyes.

'It'll probably come to that,' she said.

CHAPTER FOURTEEN

Rufus went out of the back door, round the side of the house, and walked back to school the way he had come. The streets were deserted, everyone was indoors having their tea. Rufus didn't really know why he was going back to school but he knew he wanted to go.

There was no one else in the playground as he crossed it, the main entrance stood open and Rufus walked in. He walked down the empty corridors and school seemed a safe place, somehow a dear place, with familiar pictures on the walls and where things stayed the same. You obeyed the rules and could expect to be treated in a certain way. He could not bear to think about what his mum had said, about what it might mean. Keeping his mind carefully blank he walked down to his empty classroom, opened the blue door, went in and sat down at his desk. He was waiting, but he didn't know what for.

In the staff room the meeting ended. The Headmaster had been complimentary about the funds raised for UNICEF, if less than enthusiastic about the spectacle of the children themselves. Mr Carmichael felt satisfied as he wished the other members of staff goodnight and a pleasant weekend.

He walked with his long easy stride to the form room to collect the weekend marking. He threw open the door, took one pace inside and saw Rufus sitting silently at his desk. The boy looked white-faced, calm and shocked.

Mr Carmichael took in the scene swiftly, went to Rufus, took a chair and sat down opposite him.

'What's up, Rufus?' he asked softly.

'They're getting divorced,' replied Rufus.

'Your parents?'

Rufus nodded. His eyes were filled with fear beneath the forgotten hat.

Mr Carmichael looked grim, but his voice was gentle and kind.

'I'm so sorry. Have you just found this out?'

Rufus nodded. Tears welled up in his eyes.

'I hoped you'd be here,' he said.

'I'm glad I was.'

Mr Carmichael found the Headmaster who rang to tell Mum where Rufus was and that they would bring him home. He then fetched Rufus a hot chocolate from the machine and sat down opposite him as he drank it.

'Do you want to talk about it, Rufus?'

Rufus shrugged. 'Don't mind.'

He looked up into Mr Carmichael's nice brown eyes.

'I think this has been going on for a while, hasn't it?'

Rufus nodded. 'Ever since I can remember. I can't remember a time when it was all right, when they didn't argue.'

'Not much fun for you.'

Rufus shook his head. 'I never ask Eddie round because of that. His mum and dad laugh and muck about all the time. Mine just hate each other.'

'Hard for you to work as well.'

Rufus nodded in agreement. He looked up and Mr Carmichael saw the stark fear in his eyes. 'Dad's moving out,' he said.

Mr Carmichael considered this. 'Is he going far away?'

'Mum says he's going to live with somebody else, some ... friend. I don't know who it is. He's going to leave Mum and me behind. I keep thinking perhaps it's because I didn't get very good marks ...'

Mr Carmichael cut in swiftly:

'No! It's not your fault, Rufus, it's nothing to do with what *you've* done or not done. It's an adult matter, between adults. Now listen. Some men and women are lucky. Some, like Eddie's parents, meet the right person and they're happy together, and get along fine. Other couples *think* they've met the right person, but they realise afterwards that they've just made a mistake, we *all* make mistakes. It *felt* like the right person but in actual fact it *wasn't*.

'Well, then they've got two choices, they can either let the situation drag on, and live together and hate doing it OR they can agree to undo that bit. To just say "we took the wrong turning". You ever been in a maze, Rufus?'

Rufus nodded. 'Hampton Court,' he said.

'Well, I think life's a bit like a maze. Sometimes people choose the wrong way. They come to a dead end, they're trapped, they can't move on. Some people decide to turn round and come back. Try another path. It sounds sensible but it's hard, Rufus, it's hard for everybody, especially for children stuck in the middle like you are, who always think it's *their* fault when it isn't. But, if you *can* struggle through it, you may find at the end of the day, that your parents are actually a lot happier apart than they are now when they're fighting all the time.'

Rufus listened, unconvinced. Something occurred to him. 'Are you divorced?' he asked.

Mr Carmichael nodded. 'Yes. I had no children, though. It was easier in that respect.'

Rufus laced his fingers around the plastic cup of hot chocolate. Mr Carmichael reminded him of other children in Form 3 whose parents were divorced, and Rufus thought about them. The twins Nick and Sam Diamond. Sarah Day too, who always went on about having two holidays a year.

But he didn't want to be like them. Not at all. He wanted his own home, everything as it had always been. He couldn't understand why anything had to change, couldn't make sense of it at all. He felt overwhelmingly tired.

'I'll run you home if you like, Rufus,' said Mr Carmichael. There was concern in his voice. He saw that Rufus's arms below the blood-spattered sleeves were cold and goose-pimpled.

CHAPTER FIFTEEN

Mr Carmichael took him home in his car. Subdued as he was, Rufus could not fail to notice the interior. The dashboard was full of dials and there were buttons with clever shapes so that he ached to press them. He sank into the seat, breathed in the smell of the leather and stared out at the grey bonnet.

The ride was brutally short and in only a few minutes they were parked in front of his house. Dad's car was still absent. Mum wrenched open the front door. She looked frail and worried. She stepped down, put an arm around Rufus's shoulders and invited Mr Carmichael inside.

Rufus went up to his bedroom. Downstairs he could discern a low mumble as Mum and Mr Carmichael talked. He heard Mum filling the kettle.

The Nubbler liked to make a kind of nest in Rufus's beanbag, and he was waiting there, listening on the black headset. As the bedroom door opened he took the headset off and placed it back round his neck.

Rufus felt unutterably weary. He pushed off his shoes, threw the crocodile hat into the corner and lay down upon his bed.

'Not much longer now,' said the Nubbler, sitting down on the floor beside him.

'What d'you mean?' Rufus asked.

'Well, things'll get better now.'

'They're going to get divorced.'

'I know they are. You won't like it. But afterwards it'll be better.'

'After what?'

'After your dad goes.'

Rufus was aghast. 'Better?' His voice was raised, incredulous, he was half in tears. 'How can it be better? I don't want Dad to go! Why's Dad got to go? Where's he supposed to be going?'

'Not far,' the Nubbler said quietly, 'you'll still see him. And you'll like it better then. He'll be happy.'

'I don't understand!' Rufus shouted. 'I don't understand all this! Why would he be happy without us?'

The thought of his dad going away was like a punch in the stomach.

The Nubbler was staring at him with his big eyes, as though trying to decide something. Finally he lifted his head as if he had made up his mind.

'I'm going to show you something, Rufus,' he said, 'and you may not understand it. Just look at it, and notice how all the people seem to feel and then if ever you get frightened, you can remember it and it'll help you.'

'Are we going away?' Rufus asked.

'Well, it's a bit different this time. And it isn't yet, Rufus. It's not for some time. Don't try to talk to any of the people because ... well, because they can't see you.'

'What, I'm *invisible*! Am I *invisible*?' Rufus gasped.

The Nubbler shrugged. 'Well, something like that. And don't run about, you'll scare the chickens.'

'Can the chickens see me?'

'Mmmm. Now get under the cover. Close your eyes. Just watch. Watch.'

He was on a lawn. It was warm and sunny. There were chickens around his feet. Beside him was a white-painted house and a big greenhouse with the sun flashing brilliantly on the roof. The big sliding door was rolled open and a man came out into the sunshine. It was a moment before Rufus realised it was Dad. He looked so different. His face had lost the grey, strained look and he had somehow filled out. Instead of his usual tired black suit, he was wearing a green boilersuit, sort of working clothes. He stood in the sunshine, relaxed, wiping his hands on a cloth. Suddenly a grey-haired woman he did not know came out of the white house and walked over to Dad.

'He's still coming, isn't he?' said Dad anxiously.

'Don't worry, he's coming,' the woman said, smiling. 'I just came to tell you his eggs have started hatching.'

Dad grinned a big pleased grin. He came away from the greenhouse, stood close to the woman and put both his hands on her shoulders.

'What? In the incubator?'

The lady nodded. 'Yep. You can hear them cheeping. What about that for planning?'

Dad looked so happy, it was unbelievable. 'Thanks, Eunice, he'll be thrilled. You wait till you see his face. Come on, let's go and have a look.'

The woman looked happy as well. Dad put his free arm round her shoulders and together they walked towards the house. Rufus felt baffled and uneasy.

A car was coming down the drive. Dad heard it, stopped and turned. He removed his arm from Eunice's shoulders, left her by the front door and hurried back. The car glided to a stop and a boy got out. A bigger boy, holding a bag. Rufus could not see his face. The boy rushed up to Dad, flung the bag down and hugged him. They were laughing and over-joyed to see each other. There were a few shouts of greeting and the dark car drove away. The boy still had his back to Rufus.

'You all right, son? Had a good week?' It was Dad like he had never seen him, happy and friendly, even suntanned.

The boy was nodding and chattering excitedly.

Eunice had joined them. 'How's Mum? How's Mum and Sean?'

The boy said, 'Fine, fine, they're going to see a film. How about you? You sell anything at the show?'

'All the clematis!' Eunice nodded brightly. 'It was really good.'

'And you want to check that incubator!' Dad was saying with a pleased, I-know-something-that-you-don't, grin.

'My eggs? Have they hatched out? Have I got some chicks?' he heard the boy gasp.

'You go and have a look in your room. You go and have a look,' Dad said, 'Eunice timed it just about right!'

Then a chilling thing happened. The boy turned and ran forwards, laughing. Rufus suddenly felt the Nubbler's steady-ing hand on his arm as he stared into the boy's face. It was him. It was Rufus.

Downstairs Mr Carmichael stood up to leave. He sensed that Mum wanted to say something else.

'Mr Carmichael, there's just one other thing ...'

'Yes?'

She was uncomfortable. 'Well, I can't be sure but ... once or twice ...' She paused.

Mr Carmichael waited in his calm way.

'Have you noticed Rufus talking to himself?' Mum burst out.

'Talking to himself.' He thought about it. He remembered something strange about the first time he had talked to the boy, that morning when he'd forgotten his homework.

'Not exactly, no. Why do you ask?'

'Well, when he's up in his bed I hear him talking some nights. Just chatting away to someone. It's a bit eerie.'

'Any particular nights?'

Mum looked guilty. 'When there's been a row. Mostly,' she admitted. 'I wondered if he'd invented some sort of imaginary friend, you know, to comfort him.' She looked sad.

Mr Carmichael nodded.

'It's possible. It certainly wouldn't be unusual. I think he's under considerable strain.'

After Mr Carmichael had gone, Mum went up to Rufus's room where again she felt uneasy. Rufus was in bed dressed in the crocodile T-shirt. He was fast asleep but his face was working in a strange way. At first she thought he was crying but when she bent softly over him she could see that in fact it was a smile that came and went on his sleeping face, and she noticed that his hands were cupped. There was nothing inside them at all, but they were cupped so tenderly round the emptiness that it was almost as if he was holding some small, fragile creature.

CHAPTER SIXTEEN

It was obvious that his parents had discussed divorce because the atmosphere changed at home and the rows came to an abrupt halt. This did not mean that it was pleasant there because it was not. There was a horrible sense of home being neither one thing nor the other. Rufus did not ask questions because he was afraid of hearing the answers. Dad seemed to be doing more long trips than usual.

One afternoon Rufus came in from school to find Mum and Dad seated at the kitchen table talking. There was a queer atmosphere of finality over them, as though they were discussing a death. They broke off when he came in and started doing other things.

Dad was different. All the anger had gone out of him and he looked sheepish and guilty. Once or twice he paused when they passed each other, as though he wanted to talk to Rufus but then he'd hear Mum clink something in the kitchen and think better of it. There was this tangible sense of waiting. Rufus found he actually preferred to be at school.

His parents had readily agreed to pay for the skiing trip, which had surprised him. He had not had to plead or use any persuasion at all.

CHAPTER SEVENTEEN

On a Saturday morning three weeks later the school minibus, driven by Mr Carmichael, drew into the car park of the Dry Ski Centre near Gloucester. Mr Carmichael turned to address the newly-formed Skiing Club crouching excitedly in the back.

'Make no mistake,' he said, 'you will fall over. But listen to what is said to you, keep going even though you may be discouraged at first and you will soon discover one of the best sports of all. A few lessons here will make a huge difference when we get to the snow. All right? Any questions?'

Frantic shaking of heads.

'Right. You go in that door there and wait, in an ORDERLY fashion, for your instructor.'

Except for Jude, who waited to walk in beside Mr Carmichael, they swarmed up the steps and battled through the door.

Inside was a reception desk and a bright shop selling skiing gear. Rachel, who loved clothes, dived into the racks of ski outfits, Rufus, Eddie and Anthony rushed round the display of glossy skis, Nick and Sam Diamond consumed the holiday posters with Ian Watson, Sarah and the others. There was a hubbub of noise and a sense of nervousness and excitement.

The surface of the dry ski slope was like stiff upturned scrubbing brushes arranged in a diamond pattern. Nozzles were placed at intervals alongside it, and these took it in turn to soak the surface with powerful jets of water. At last the would-be skiers of Form 3 spilled out on to the slope. They were red-faced from bending to coax their feet into the stiff, hard-to-fasten boots. All walked awkwardly, clutching the heavy skis, peering up the dramatic slope with worried faces. It was of undreamed-of steepness. Mr Carmichael, who knew how to ski, leaned on a barrier to watch.

Their instructor was called Harry. He wore a large red hat and a blue knee brace. Sarah Day was disappointed because she had been led to understand by her girl friends that all ski instructors were romantic-looking and heroic. She studied Harry's blue knee brace and thought again.

He gave them a talk about the various parts of their skis, then they had to put them on, form a line and walk sideways in tiddly steps up the lower section of the slope. Then, and this was the frightening bit, they had to walk out, face down the slope and glide down on their skis. At least, it frightened the others. Yet when Rufus faced down the slope, although he had never been taught, from somewhere the ability just came to him. Skis parallel he leaned forward, almost kneeling in the strong grey boots. Perfectly balanced, he glided down to the start.

'Yeah, well, he's done it before!' Harry shouted to the others. 'Watch him, he's good, that's what you're after.'

Rufus took his place back in the line. He could tell that the others had been impressed. Yet he hadn't done it before. Not

60

really. Had he? It was really weird. He felt a small congratulatory poke in the back and reached out to touch the unseen Nubbler beside him.

It soon became clear that Anthony Wan was going to be good. Eddie too, because he was small and athletic. In fact, Rufus realised, three boys got the hang of it first, and they were the three from the skiing dream. Ian Watson came to grief. He couldn't believe it was right to lean forward so he leaned back, his skis shot out in front of him and he went backwards on to his bottom. His thumb stuck down into the bristled surface and twisted painfully backwards. Feeling a real fool he fought back tears and glanced quickly over at Mr Carmichael, hoping he had not seen. To his relief he saw that their form teacher was staring fixedly at something in the opposite direction.

Suddenly the lesson was over and they all felt cheated by the speed with which it had passed. Another group came stumbling out of the boot-changing area and lined up waiting for Harry. Mr Carmichael looking eminently well satisfied, escorted them out amid howls that they were only just starting to *get* it!

Back in the school playground they climbed out of the bus, their legs already stiffening up. Parents waiting round a few cars greeted the children good-humouredly and claimed their own. Mr Carmichael drove the bus away and Rufus set off to walk home.

As he approached his front door he felt the Nubbler beside him. He couldn't see him, of course, but he always knew when he was there. Reaching the door he felt the Nubbler's hand on his and knew he was being prepared for something. Something bad.

Rufus pushed open the door and at first could not see

anything different. There was a rack for coats on the wall and seeing so few clothes on it he thought perhaps Mum had tidied up. Then when he looked more closely he saw there were only coats belonging to him and Mum.

All Dad's coats had gone.

He turned to look beside the front door. Dad's big work books had gone. His briefcase had gone. His walking shoes. His old trainers for doing the garden in the summer. He turned, searching for Mum. She was framed in the kitchen door and she was keeping herself very calm.

'He's gone, Rufus,' she said, 'your dad's gone.'

Rufus walked past her into the sitting-room. Dad's hi-fi had gone and his rack for cassettes and CDs. Some of the things from the shelves were missing and the silver cups he had won at school.

'He never said cheerio,' Rufus said.

'He's coming tonight to take you for a McDonalds. He'll talk to you about it.'

'Where's he gone, Mum? Where's he actually gone?'

'Well, I told you, your dad's got a friend, Rufus,' Mum said, trying to keep her voice even, trying to keep out the bitterness she felt.

'He's known her for a long time. She's got a market garden I believe. Sort of a nursery, growing plants. Your dad used to know her a long time ago and then he met her again. He just … likes her better than me, Rufus, it's as simple as that.

'So, Dad came in today and cleared out his things and he has gone over to her, as far as I know. She lives at Chadworth. I don't know her name. She's got some money, I think. I suppose she's better looking than me. And younger too I expect.'

Rufus was trying to be helpful and spoke without thinking.

'No she's not, Mum. Her name's Eunice and she's old, older than you and she's got grey hair.'

Mum stared at him, open-mouthed. 'WHAT? How on *earth* do you know that?' she gasped.

He ran past her in confusion, quickly up to his bedroom and slammed the door. It was getting hard to remember what was real.

CHAPTER EIGHTEEN

Mr Carmichael, who also taught Drama, sat at home reading plays in search of one the school could do for Christmas. Several books lay discarded and now he was looking with increasing optimism through a script of *The Arabian Nights*. These ancient folk tales might do very well, he thought. Woven in them was a cave full of jewels, Sindbad the Sailor, the legendary queen Scheherazade, forty thieves and even, if required, Aladdin and his magic lamp. At least everybody would have a part.

He closed the book, well pleased, and leaned back considering how to imbue the creaking stage with the perfumed mysteries of the East. They would need two backcloths, a forest for the poor woodcutter and a courtyard for Sindbad's grand palace. He knew just the boy to paint them for him.

Mr Carmichael knew Rufus Clark's father had now moved out of the family home, and considered how the boy must feel, knowing his father would never live there again. Painting an Eastern backcloth could take up a lot of time. It could take up a lot of evenings and weekends. Why, with all the ornate windows and wrought ironwork, it was the kind of job which could prevent a boy from sitting about brooding at home for weeks.

CHAPTER NINETEEN

They faced each other across a pale table in McDonalds.
Between them was the cardboard carrying tray containing
the burgers, Rufus's milk shake and Dad's coffee. There were a
few customers dotted about, a youth in a cap was sweeping
the floor, otherwise it was pretty quiet.

'I don't suppose you think much of your dad, Rufus.'

Rufus shrugged. He felt so many different things. He felt
like clinging on to his dad and pleading with him not to go.
At other times when he thought about it and realised that
Dad was just going, just walking out on him and Mum as if
they were nothing, then he felt angry. Then anger boiled up
and he would have liked to punch his dad, hit him and hurt
him. He couldn't say any of this. He just shrugged again.

'It was Mum who called it all off, son,' Dad said.

'Oh yeah, blame Mum!' Rufus spat out. He could see that
Dad was shocked at the contempt in his raised voice. 'It's all
Mum's fault, I suppose. How come you were always making
her cry!'

Dad's eyes flicked round the restaurant, embarrassed. The
youth in the cap was watching them with interest.

'I don't mean that!' he hissed. 'What I'm trying to say is

that I admire her for it. Well, nobody was happy were they? You, me, Mum, none of us were happy. I would have let it drag on, that's what I'm trying to say. You know ... the situation. But only because it was easiest. I'm saying Mum was brave.' His words petered out weakly. He was floundering. Beads of sweat appeared and merged together on his upper lip.

Rufus stared at his dad in exasperation and despair. He loved him and hated him. The solution seemed so simple, so blindingly obvious.

'Don't go, Dad. Why don't you just come back and not argue any more?'

'I can't son. It's all gone too far. You'll understand when you're older ...'

'I'm sick of hearing that!' Rufus muttered.

Dad was breathing heavily and appeared at a complete loss. Suddenly he looked at a point behind Rufus and his face cleared. The anguish dissolved and was replaced by pure relief.

'Look, I want you to meet Eunice, Rufus, she's been my ... friend for a long time. I wanted you to meet her right away and get it over with. She's here now ...'

Dad had made a big mistake.

Rufus did not look up as she sat down at their table. It was queer knowing what she looked like already. Where was the Nubbler? He wasn't around. Rufus wished he was.

'Hello Rufus,' Eunice said.

Rufus looked up and stared at her. She looked frightened to death. She had grotty grey hair and she was old and nothing like as pretty as Mum. He didn't answer her.

'I hope we'll all be able to be friends, Rufus ...' she stumbled on, 'and your dad and I ...'

She suddenly covered Dad's hand with her own. She sat there holding Dad's hand just like that! Rufus snapped. He felt a red tide of furious anger rising up his neck, up through his face. He bunched his fist, raised it and brought it down as hard as he could on their two entwined hands. Eunice gasped with pain and shock.

Rufus sprang to his feet, shouting. 'NO! NO! I'm not being friends with YOU! You get out! You leave my dad alone! He's not yours! Why don't you leave us alone!'

Eunice put her bruised hand to her mouth. She bowed her head and began to cry silently. Everyone had turned to look. The manager appeared and hovered, watching.

Rufus wanted to hurt them as much as they had hurt him. He had been pushed too far and had snapped. Staring desperately round the table he noticed the carrying tray still untouched. With furious anger and strength he swiped it at his father. The hot coffee shot in a brown tide over the white table and whacked into Dad's chest. Then Rufus shoved past him, hating them, and ran out into the street.

CHAPTER TWENTY

It took him a long time to walk home. Down a succession of wintry streets he went and trees confined in the cold pavement rattled their bare branches over his head like bones.

The icy wind cooled his red face. He had exploded. All the fear and worry and tension had blown up like a bomb. Now he felt quite calm, and older. He felt as though they had rushed him into being older. He wasn't even sorry about the coffee. It had shown Dad something of what they had done to him, how deeply they had hurt him, and hurt him by hurting Mum, and how frightened, lonely and desperate they had made him feel.

At home the front door stood open. He did not think about this but went straight in and up the stairs of the silent house. In his bedroom the Nubbler was listening on the black headset. He removed it thoughtfully as Rufus entered.

'I'm in trouble now,' he said.

'It'll be all right.'

'What? I only threw coffee at Dad! And I punched their hands!'

69

'They won't mind all that much. They'll think they deserved it.'

Rufus sat down limply on the bed. He felt exhausted.

'What am I going to do, Nubbler?' he asked.

'Don't worry. The worst is over.'

'Is it? Really?'

The Nubbler nodded, very sure. His big eyes roamed over Rufus, over his weary fallen shoulders and dirty shoes, over his worn-out face. He put his hand over Rufus's and Rufus felt a sleepiness that was as sweet as honey sweep through him. He prised off his shoes and rolled under the covers.

'Know what you need, Rufus?'

'What?'

'A pick-me-up.'

'What's a pick-me-up?' asked Rufus, sleepy but interested.

'Well, for example, a nice visit to your uncle.'

Rufus groaned. He thought of Dad's brother, Uncle Eric who called him 'my old fruit' and watched horse-racing on TV all the time. Or his wife, Auntie Shirley, who kept on about her weight and never ate anything.

'No thanks,' he said.

There was a spinning of bright colours before him. Rufus sat up, astounded. A great vortex of turquoise, white and gold whirled before his eyes. Thrown off balance he stretched out his hands, swaying. In his ears he could hear the sound of gulls, splashes, shouts of joy. In his mouth he could taste salt air and on his skin warm sunshine suddenly soaked and drenched him like a balm. The wheel stopped turning. The colours flattened out and formed a scene.

A vast turquoise sea stretched sparkling to the horizon. In brilliant sunshine Rufus stood on the warm, bleached boards of a floating pontoon. Water slapped at the edges. Rising up beside him was a dazzling white catamaran. It rocked gently in its moorings, the wind jingling in its mast, the white sides patterned with dancing honeycombs of reflected light. Gulls turned and squabbled in the air overhead.

There were people all around him, laughing and happy in bright bathing costumes. Some in diving gear and flippers were seated at the edge of the pontoon, carefully falling backwards into the sea.

A man with ringing footsteps came striding across the planks towards Rufus. He was wearing a broad grin. Kneeling on the baked wood he took him warmly by the shoulders. The laughing eyes Rufus remembered so well shone with pleasure. On his jaw there was a port-wine birthmark.

'Hello, Roof!'

It was Uncle Allan. They were in Australia.

'You hungry, mate?' he asked.

Rufus shook his head in wonderment.

'Well, come on then, we haven't got long! Let's get you into this lot!'

From square bins on the pontoon Uncle Allan handed him blue flippers, a snorkel and mask. Rufus put them on.

'Here y'are mate, bite on this bit!'

Rufus clenched his teeth on the rubber mouthpiece of the snorkel.

'Don't forget Roof, breathe through your mouth! Look at what you want, but don't touch anything, it's all protected. All set?'

Rufus stood woodenly in the mask and flippers. He felt a small push in the back and nodded.

'OK,' he said.

'Hold on to my arm, Roof! Let go when you're ready!'

They were in the sea. It was luxuriously warm. He was

obediently holding Uncle Allan's thick muscular forearm, treading water and looking blankly into his uncle's masked face. He did not know what to do next.

'Well, look down, mate!' Uncle Allan shouted, laughing.

Rufus looked down into the water. What he saw there took his breath away.

Below him like a mountain range lay part of the Great Barrier Reef of Australia. A tapestry of coloured coral and waving seeweeds extended in all directions, dappled with sunlight and studded with jewel-bright fishes. Enchanted and dazzled, Rufus who was a strong swimmer, let go of his uncle's arm and struck out on his own. Sweet-faced fish swam up and peered innocently into his mask.

He allowed himself to drift over the scene, fighting down a sense of vertigo because, like mountains, the ocean floor ranged over spectacular peaks and troughs. Now he was moving over pink and yellow coral, fluted shells and velvet sea anemones close enough to touch, and next he was exposed over some black chasm where the sea bed fell away to an awesome and terrifying depth, where some unspeakable creature might lie coiled, ready to torpedo up from the dark and get him.

His uncle's presence nearby reassured him and Rufus drifted on. Exquisite stripy fish in yellows and blues, like those he had only ever seen in pet-shop aquariums, paused to look him over curiously, their lips pursed. He reached out and touched them. They flicked away casually, unafraid.

After a time Uncle Allan made pointing signs and they swam back towards the pontoon. As they came near, someone threw a bucketful of bread into the water. Assorted marine life rushed to the scene and an enormous grey fish with thick lips and an indignant expression shouldered Rufus out of the way. 'They think I'm a fish!' he thought, enchanted, 'they think I'm just another fish!'

He swam round to the aluminium steps which extended down from the pontoon. Just before he got out of the water Rufus looked around once more and saw that beside him was a little suspended group of sea-horses, their heads modestly bowed. Along their backs they had a single whirring fin, and as they peered at him with their big steady eyes, they seemed familiar. It was only as he walked towards the catamaran for lunch with his uncle that he realised that he had been looking into the face of the Nubbler.

CHAPTER TWENTY-ONE

After Rufus ran out of McDonalds, Dad put his arm round Eunice who was still crying, and together they hurried round a street corner to where Dad's car was parked. They got in and Dad phoned Mum using the car phone. She was livid with Dad for introducing Eunice too soon, and terrified that something would befall a boy not used to roaming the streets at night. They agreed to search, Mum near home and Dad and Eunice in the town, and to meet up in an hour. Mum took a coat from the empty-looking rack and ran out in such a panic that the front door was left wide open.

After an hour's fruitless search they met in the street and came indoors. Mum, wide-eyed with fear, did not acknowledge the presence of Eunice. Eunice's hand was bruised blue and swollen. Mum ran upstairs to check Rufus's bedroom and on entering it sagged with relief. He was in bed asleep. As his mother entered, Rufus opened his eyes. Far from the anger or tears she might have expected, the boy's face was a picture of full joy.

'Oh Mum,' Rufus said, 'oh Mum, these beautiful shells, look at these beautiful seashells ...'

He turned away and closed his eyes as though he couldn't

wait to go back. Mum was not sure she had heard him right. She stood perplexed, staring about her. Something made her uneasy. Apart from what Rufus had said there was a smell in the room she could not account for. It was a smell she recognised but could not explain. It was a foresty smell, like a fir-cone. Or a Christmas tree.

CHAPTER TWENTY-TWO

It was terrible coming home from school now that Dad had gone. To walk in knowing he wouldn't be there, wouldn't ask him about school, about how he did in the spelling test. Of course Rufus hadn't forgotten the rows, the shouting and tears. He didn't miss them. But there was just this huge aching space. This gap. The gap where his own dad, faults and all, had been. Mum was quiet. The house was quiet. It was as though they were all in mourning, and in a way they were.

It was cold now as winter came on. Mum switched on the central heating and the boiler didn't work properly. Rufus saw her fiddling with it ineffectually and knew she was close to tears.

At school Mr Carmichael cast the *Arabian Nights* play they would be doing for the parents at Christmas. Form 3 were reassured. The play sounded suitably bloodthirsty, with great curved scimitars and people getting stoppered up in oil jars. Sarah Day was to play Sheherazade, Anthony Wan was the Caliph, Ian Watson was Sindbad and the rest were thieves, woodgatherers and exotic-looking wives.

Mr Carmichael had asked Rufus to help with painting the

set and to check with his mother about staying on later in the evenings. Rufus was pleased. It was a better prospect than being at home missing Dad.

His parents were deciding what time he would be spending with each of them, but they could not agree. In the meantime the weeks went by and he did not see Dad. He felt uncomfortable now when he thought about the incident in McDonalds. He supposed he shouldn't have hit Eunice, she was probably perfectly all right. He didn't care if she was or not. What mattered was that she was where he so wanted Mum to be. With Dad.

It was hard for Rufus. He longed to see Dad, but he knew that Mum hated Eunice, so by wanting to see Dad he hurt Mum. He become confused and was glad to be at school slapping paint on the giant Eastern backcloth Mr Carmichael had sketched out for the play. He liked being with Mr Carmichael. Everybody liked him. He was fair, quick to laugh and always the same. One Monday evening Rufus and he were painting the courtyard backcloth together on the floor of the sports hall. From the adjoining cloakrooms came the sound of Nick and Sam Diamond washing brushes. It was their job to paint the giant brown oil jars.

'Do anything interesting over the weekend, Rufus?' asked Mr Carmichael, tracing in the wrought ironwork of the windows.

'No.'

'Are you seeing your father?'

'No. He wants to have me but Mum says she hates the thought of me being there with Eunice. She's Dad's ... friend.'

'So you're not seeing him?'

'No. At first Mum said I could see him as often as I wanted

to but now she doesn't want to talk about it. She gets mad. She calls Eunice a cow. So I haven't seen him. Not yet.' His voice trailed off.

Mr Carmichael had stopped painting the wrought iron-work. He was staring hard at Rufus. He seemed perturbed. Rufus wondered if he had said too much.

'But what do *you* want, Rufus?' he asked.

Rufus said anxiously, 'Well, I want them to get back together. That's what I want most. If I can't have that, I want to see them both. Sort of equal. But with Mum not minding. You know, not making me feel I'm doing something to hurt her if I go to see Dad. I'd love to see Dad.'

'Would you like me to talk to your mother?'

Rufus nodded eagerly. 'Yes. Yes please.'

'I don't know if it will do any good.'

'No, but you could talk to her. Tonight! Can you talk to her tonight? When you drop me off?'

Mr Carmichael thought for a moment and nodded.

'All right. I'll have a word with her tonight.'

CHAPTER TWENTY-THREE

Mum watched Mr Carmichael drive off. She picked up his coffee cup and her own, took them through into the kitchen, then went quietly upstairs to check Rufus. He was asleep, his paint-spattered hand curled next to his face. She stood staring down at him, loving him. Mr Carmichael was right, of course. Rufus only wanted to see his dad. She felt heavy with guilt. Of course she was in the wrong. Mr Carmichael hadn't said that, but just by talking to him she knew it was true.

She came downstairs and sat by herself in the sitting-room. There was a plain choice, really. She could wound Dad by withholding his son from him, nurse her feelings of bitterness and revenge, continue to hate the plain Eunice and do what she could to make their lives a misery. There would be some pleasure in that, the pleasure of revenge, of getting her own back.

On the other hand she could put Rufus first, fight down the hostility she felt herself and try to let her boy travel freely and good-naturedly between his parents. She could try to form some sort of working relationship with Dad and Eunice and endeavour to build a new life for herself.

The trouble was she didn't know where to start. Mr Carmichael said they needed help with the play costumes. Scheherazade needed a veil, and the Caliph a fancy turban.

Impulsively she picked up the phone and dialled the number Dad had left. She was nervous and her heart beat fast but she had decided that Rufus could go and see them. She hated giving them this concession but Rufus was the one who mattered. He hadn't done anything wrong and was longing to see his dad.

So it was that the following weekend Rufus went to visit his father and Eunice for the first time. Mum had bought him a bag, a large zippered green sports bag for weekends, she said. She packed a set of clean clothes and his wellington boots because, as she told him, it was a farm sort of place and there would no doubt be muck.

At ten o'clock on Saturday morning Dad pulled up outside in his salesman's car. Inside the house she fiercely hugged Rufus, gave him a big kiss and a bright smile. She stood at the door and smiled and waved as her son went off to be looked after for the day by Eunice.

When they were lost to view the smile crumbled from her face, she closed the door of the silent house and sank down on the stairs, aghast. It was agony to see him go, to let him go. What if he liked Eunice? What if he came to like Eunice better than her? She sat in tears on the stairs, hugging her knees and rocking herself gently.

After a long time she got to her feet and caught sight of herself in the hall mirror. She looked frightful, her face red and swollen from crying.

On the shelf above the hall mirror stood a white polystyrene head, used to display hats at the shop. She reached up, took it down and looked at it this way and that.

Upstairs, still carrying the head, she dragged out a box of fabric scraps she'd accumulated from work. Pretty remnants nobody had bought, but which she felt were far too beautiful to throw away. She felt down into the box and pulled up a handful of pieces at random. There was a shiny blue silk with gold threads. Mum draped it round the head, turban-fashion.

CHAPTER TWENTY-FOUR

Of course the farm belonging to Eunice was the same place that the Nubbler had shown him. In Dad's car they drove up to the white house. Rufus could see the greenhouse exactly where it had been in the dream and it occurred to him that it was some time since he last saw the Nubbler. Not since the pick-me-up. Somehow he had been really busy since then. He was doing the set for the play in the evenings and Skiing Club at weekends. Usually he only saw the Nubbler to talk to when he was alone and worried in his bedroom, and lately he had hardly been there.

It was true that Rufus was nervous when they stopped outside Eunice's house. The last encounter hadn't exactly been a triumph, but sitting there this time, next to his dad, he felt stronger and better. Dad was nervous too, Rufus could tell. But things had become clearer. Things had calmed down. They sat side by side in the car after the long separation.

'Look Rufus,' Dad began.

'What, Dad?' he replied. The word stood out comfortingly.

'Look, I can't tell you how to do this, but ... she's not trying to be Mum. Eunice isn't. She's not trying to be ...

instead of Mum. She knows you've got your own, good mum. All she wants ... all she wants is to be friends. See? She would like to be friends with you. Not straight away, not artificial. After a bit. After we've all got to know each other ... See, son?'

Rufus nodded. 'OK, Dad.'

They got out of the car. Dad leaned in and collected the green sports bag with the wellington boots sticking out of the top. Together they went towards the front door. It suddenly opened. Eunice was there but bursting past her came a big cream-coloured retriever dog. He bounded round Rufus and barked in a large voice. Rufus was amazed to see the beautiful dog and reached out to him with both hands. The dog launched himself at Rufus and slapped a great wet lick across his face. Rufus put his fingers in the long silky hair, laughing, turning away from the slapping tongue. Dad was laughing and as Rufus struggled to his feet he saw Eunice was too.

'Hello, Rufus,' she said.

'Hello,' he replied.

Dad put his arm round his shoulders and they all walked into the white house.

'What's your dog's name?' he asked Eunice.

'Twit,' she said.

It seemed an indignity for such a fine dog. 'Why d'you call him Twit?' he asked.

Dad and Eunice said together, 'Because he *is* a twit!'

In the kitchen there were cakes and biscuits and juice and they sat about for a while, not knowing what to say. It was awkward. Then Dad said they had got a room ready for him because they hoped, not today of course, but they hoped he would come to stay for weekends and whenever he wanted, once everything was sorted out. Would he like to see it?

He went upstairs with Dad. They went past a closed bedroom door and Rufus suddenly realised that his dad probably slept in there with Eunice. It gave him a horrible gut feeling to think of his dad close to someone else and not at home in his own bed with Mum. Suddenly the whole thing began to turn bad. He felt he didn't want to be here, he shouldn't be here, it was all wrong. Torn between his mum and dad, he stopped half-way along the landing. At that point he felt the Nubbler beside him. He felt the little webbed fingers on his arm and a small push in the back. Just a minor, encouraging sort of push. Just to say go on give it a try. The Nubbler was there. It was all right. The Nubbler was there with him.

Rufus had to admit that it was a nice room. Old houses were different. At home the walls were square and the floors level, but here the floor sloped and the ceilings came low down on to the walls. The window was low too, to see out properly you had to kneel on the floor. Just outside there was a tree. It was old and the branches were thick. Rufus thought you could probably climb out of the window straight into the tree.

'Know what I was thinking?' asked Dad.

'What?'

'I was thinking you could put a treehouse out there ...'

'What, outside the window?'

'Well, back a bit. Could be done ...'

Rufus looked round the room. There was a washbasin on the wall and a neat single bed.

'We didn't get you a duvet. We thought you might like to bring one from home. Or I saw one the other day with the Red Arrows on. I could get you that if you want.'

Inside, secretly, Rufus let go of the breath he had been

holding on to and sighed a deep, tentative sigh of relief. Perhaps it wasn't going to be so bad. His dad *had* moved away but Rufus could come too, whenever he wanted, and this was the room he could stay in. Dad *had* left Mum to live with another woman but that woman was only Eunice and she did have Twit. For the first time, he began to see that the future might not be the nightmare he had feared. He might, he just might be able to cope with it, if it didn't get any worse than this.

In the room there was a foresty smell. Dad might have thought it came from the tree outside the window, but it did not.

At home Mum looked up at the clock. Five o'clock. He would be home in an hour. She looked back at what she was doing and felt a considerable touch of pride. Festooned about the white head was a glorious turban. She had stitched the blue and gold fabric into position, padded it, added several more drapes of rich material and swathes of old pearly beads. Finding the front part of a vast green rhinestone brooch from a long-dead granny, she had stitched this on as the centre-piece.

The overall effect was stunning. A Caliph would die of pride wearing this. She smiled, and peering into the long-forgotten box spotted a piece of purple velvet. She yanked it out and added it, twisting and turning it to the best advantage. There was no doubt, it was stupendous. In due course she would transport it to school and bestow it upon Mr Carmichael.

She froze as she heard Dad's car, then rushed to the door. The car door slammed and she heard Rufus's footsteps running eagerly up the path. She opened the door, waved briefly, ushered him in and looked him over. He looked happy. Determined to try hard she hugged him and said 'How'd it go?'

It was hard to listen to. The room was fantastic, the chickens and incubators were fantastic, the big greenhouse, the terrific dog, how they had a pond with frogs in it, the treehouse Dad talked about, they'd got fish and chips on the way home ...

Mum was jealous and frightened of losing him. She wondered if Dad and Eunice were going to try to take Rufus away from her completely. The smile disappeared from her face. They went into the sitting-room.

'MUM!' Rufus gasped.

'What?' She was startled.

'Did YOU make THIS?' He was gazing in awe at the turban.

'Yes,' laughed Mum. 'I made it while you were gone.'

'It's FANTASTIC! Oh, it's FANTASTIC, Mum!'

'Oh, I'm good for something then!' she said.

Rufus hugged her and his face was lit up as she had not seen it for months, both with relief at the way the day had gone, and with pride in the turban. 'You're good for EVERYTHING, Mum!' he protested.

This small exchange made Mum feel better.

CHAPTER TWENTY-FIVE

Outside the classroom window the scene was gloomy. Fog drifted aimlessly over the school grounds and dead spiky garden. Mr Carmichael was taking them for art. They were talking about ways to depict the sea.

'What do you know about the *Titanic*?' he asked. 'Malcolm, can you tell us anything?'

'Yeah, it sunk, sir,' replied Malcolm Keen with a smirk.

'What was it? Why did it sink?' asked Mr Carmichael sharply.

'A ship. Hit a iceberg.'

'Correct. Hit *an* iceberg. But why did it cause such a sensation? Apart from the huge loss of life, why was it so remarkable? Anyone?'

Ian Watson's arm flapped madly. 'I know sir! I know!'

'Watson?'

'It was on its maiden voyage, sir!'

'And what is a maiden voyage? Were there only maidens on it?'

'No, it was new, sir, it had never sailed anywhere before,' Sarah Day offered sensibly.

'And it was ever so big, sir,' said Jude.

'Thank you, Jude, it was vast. It was new. It was hailed as the most modern ship of all time. And what was the one word they used to describe it? Anybody?'

'Unsinkable,' called Rufus.

'Yes, they said it was unsinkable. But on its maiden voyage, through the freezing cold waters of the North Atlantic, it struck an iceberg and sank. There were parties on board. People were celebrating. Remember it was the maiden voyage of a ship *half as big again* as anything which had ever sailed.

'Everyone was dressed up, they would have had the finest food, entertainment, orchestras. And then this brightly lit ship, all pleasure and gilt and sumptuous luxury, ploughed into an iceberg. There was a ten second grinding impact. Think about it. Think about the change. No one came to help. In two hours and forty minutes the whole thing slid into the freezing cold, black sea. It disappeared. It had too few lifeboats.

'Over fifteen hundred people were left, little tiny specks in the sea under great icebergs broken off from the Greenland glacier. Think what the scene might have looked like. Try to imagine it for one minute ...'

A shudder went through them as they thought about the people in the icy sea, people wearing jewellery, their silks and satins sodden with water. To see the lights of their ship slipping under water for ever, leaving them alone in the huge empty swell of the sea.

'Draw a picture of it, please,' instructed Mr Carmichael, knowing they were raring to go. 'Draw a picture of any aspect of the subject.'

'Can I do it being launched?' asked Nick Diamond.

'Is that an aspect of the subject?'

'Um. Yes.'

'Thank you.'

'Sir?'

'Yes, Eddie?'

'Sir, do they know where it is?'

'The *Titanic*? Oh yes.'

'Have they had divers on it?'

'I don't know, Eddie, it's a long way down. Robot submersibles went down in the eighties, things were recovered.'

'What, dead bodies?'

'I think not. Money and jewels were brought up. A lot of people thought the ship should have been left undisturbed, as a grave. You're interested, Eddie, why don't you research it, see what you can find out.'

Eddie nodded cheerfully.

Rachel at the back said, 'Sir, how old do you have to be to go diving? I mean proper diving, not just off a board.'

'Sub-aqua diving?'

'Yeah!' She was full of enthusiasm and all of them waited keenly for the answer.

'Twelve, I think. Why, are you interested?'

'Yes!' they chorused.

'Why?'

'Well, we might find some treasure!'

'Skeletons!'

Mr Carmichael studied their excited faces. 'Of course you could be lucky enough to find another Nanking cargo.'

'What? What was that, sir?'

'A load of crockery!'

They groaned.

'Don't groan, it was sold for millions. Everybody wanted it because it had been so long under the sea. It had an exotic history, you see.' He thought briefly. 'Of course there are numerous wrecks around the British coast. Who thinks they might be interested in a Wreck Diving Club?'

A forest of arms shot up.

'Well, you're not old enough yet. There's certainly a lower age limit.'

They groaned.

'But ...'

They watched him eagerly.

'It might be possible to make some sort of a start, go snorkelling say. Some schools go down to Dirdle Dore. We'd have to round up a group of helpers, need lifejackets of course, perhaps make a weekend of it in the summer ... Has anyone here done any snorkelling?'

Rufus gasped with enthusiasm and was about to fire his arm into the air, to spill out the unforgettable things he had seen on the Barrier Reef, but a small restraining hand held his arm close by his side. It hadn't been real. It had only been a pick-me-up.

Mr Carmichael had noticed the movement. 'You, Rufus?'

Rufus swallowed and then said with certainty: 'No sir, but my uncle lives in Australia, and he goes diving on the Barrier Reef, and I'm going to save up and go out there as well.'

Malcolm Keen made a scoffing noise but Mr Carmichael said: 'Good for you, Rufus. You've got the one thing that everybody needs. An ambition.' He looked at the clock on the classroom wall and flinched. 'Right! Leave this diving club idea with me then. I'll speak to the Headmaster and track down some information. And now, the *Titanic* please. Sam, give out some cartridge paper.'

At the end of the school day they poured out of the double doors. It was Friday and the mood was joyous. Rufus was surprised to see Mum waiting by the school gate. She was carrying a plastic bag.

'Mum? What're you doing?' asked Rufus.

'I finished the turban. I thought I'd walk down with it as it's a bit fragile and won't stand any rough treatment. Where's Mr Carmichael now?'

'In our form room. Mum can I just show it to Eddie? Can I just show him the turban? And Anthony? Look, Anthony, here's your hat!'

They gathered round and peered into the bag. Mum would not let them take it out, but closed it up firmly and marched off into school.

She tapped at the door of the form room.

'Come in,' called Mr Carmichael.

Mum stood in the doorway clutching the bag. 'I had a go at making the hat,' she said.

He sprang up and walked over. She took it out of the bag. The pearls clinked sweetly together. The rhinestone flashed against the blue silk with gold threads.

'This,' said Mr Carmichael in a wondering voice, 'is a work of art!'

CHAPTER TWENTY-SIX

That night Rufus was in bed. A number of things made him feel happy. Mum was bolstered by the success of the turban and was now downstairs making a diaphanous veil for Scheherazade. She was in a good mood and her sewing machine was whirring softly.

Rufus was going to Dad at the weekend and he would see Twit. He loved Twit already and Twit was ecstatic when he saw Rufus because it meant that for once he had someone to play with. Eunice said Twit had gone off her now because she didn't know any good games.

Christmas was coming and Rufus was having a complete set of skiing clothes. He had seen them in the shops and they were cool. He was having bright yellow goggles and proper padded trousers with straps up over the shoulders and a warm jacket.

He was going to ask for some of that coloured stuff that went on your nose for sunburn. He was having gloves, the long padded skiing ones, and warm furry boots because Mr Carmichael said after the day's skiing, children usually played on toboggans and so needed warm footwear. He couldn't wait. Once the school play was over, there was

Christmas and then straight after Christmas would be the skiing trip! He wriggled with pleasure and excitement at the thought.

Rufus was also pleased with the backcloth they had painted at school. The dress rehearsal was on Thursday and the backcloth was almost finished. It had looked fantastic the first time they hoisted it up. On the wall part Rufus had done a speckled effect by sloshing a wet brush at it from two paces back. He'd done it in several colours and it looked good, like real stone with lichen and stuff on.

'Hello,' said the Nubbler.

'Nubbler!' Rufus sat up. 'Where've you been?'

The Nubbler shrugged. 'Oh, on the headset,' he said vaguely. 'You look happy tonight.'

'Yes. I am. Did you see our backcloth?'

The Nubbler nodded.

'Did you know I'm getting skiing gear for Christmas? They're buying me the whole set, I didn't even have to do any jobs! Do you think they've got rich?'

The Nubbler said in a bland voice, 'No, they've got guilty.'

Rufus rushed on. 'What do you think of the turban Mum made? Even the Headmaster stopped me. He said it was excellent!'

Suddenly the Nubbler held up a webbed finger for Rufus to be quiet. Then he did a curious thing. Taking the black headset from round his neck he placed it up to his ears and began to listen intently. Rufus was taken aback and slightly affronted. Fancy deciding to listen to music right in the middle of what he was saying!

'What's your favourite band, then?' asked Rufus. The Nubbler waved the finger for silence. After a little while he took the headset off again and replaced it round his neck.

'What did you say?'

'I said what's your favourite band? Is that your favourite band you always listen to?'

The Nubbler shook his head. He looked perturbed. 'No. I've got to go now, Rufus. I'll see you on Friday. Don't worry about the hat. It'll be all right.'

With that he had gone. Rufus stared at the space in surprise. Where had he gone? And what did he mean 'Don't worry about the hat'? Rufus felt a bit cross with the Nubbler and snuggled back down into his bed. The teddy bear with the bow tie had fallen off the chair on to the floor. Feeling generous, Rufus picked him up and settled him in bed beside him.

CHAPTER TWENTY-SEVEN

It was the afternoon of the dress rehearsal and Malcolm Keen was watching the proceedings in the school hall. On the stage Rufus Clark and Mr Carmichael were fixing the backcloth. Other people were adding final dabs of paint to the scenery, adjusting little sparkling lights in the cave of jewels and trying to position the awkward one-dimensional oil jars which kept falling over.

Malcolm was on lighting and had done his bit. There were only a few spotlights on a bar on the ceiling and having angled them from the tall stepladder his job was now finished.

He was one of the few kids not going on the skiing trip. He made out he didn't want to go, of course, but being left out made something burn deep inside him. Something ugly. He hadn't even asked his dad. He knew what the answer would be.

'Yeah?' he'd sneer, 'yeah? Fancy yerself in the outfit do ya? Got plenty of money to pay for it have ya?' He'd laugh in his scornful way, and go back to reading his paper. Malcolm's cowed mother would go on working, tightlipped, and say nothing.

Malcolm's dad was a racist. He didn't think about how nice a person from another country could be, how kind or friendly. He didn't consider that it might be interesting to talk to a person from another culture and climate, or how by so doing he might even learn things to enrich his own life. In his secret soul he feared foreigners. Because their skin was a different colour, because their ways were not his ways, he saw them as a threat, hated them and taught Malcolm to hate them as well.

He said they came over here and took our people's jobs. He said if they hadn't been let in, he would probably have a job himself by now. He said they should have stayed where they came from instead of coming here, eating foreign food, living off government handouts, which meant off people like him who paid taxes, or would if they could get a job.

He said they should all have been sent back to their own countries but it was too late now, they had got too good a foothold.

Malcolm had grown up hearing his father repeat this over and over, and consequently was convinced that it was true. This was one of the reasons why Malcolm hated Anthony Wan.

Malcolm also knew Anthony was afraid of him and he liked that because it made him feel powerful and he never felt powerful at home. Furthermore by hating Anthony he was doing something his dad would approve of. His dad was not pleased with him much. He belittled him from time to time but otherwise seemed hardly to notice him at all.

Now he watched as Anthony came on stage dressed as the Caliph. Mrs Springfield, the Headmaster's wife, prided herself on the play costumes she made and was fussing around him, straightening his waistcoat, fluffing out the big sleeves,

96

fiddling with him. Malcolm watched, a mocking look on his face.

He saw her get something out of a carrier bag and put it on Anthony's head. It was a fancy turban. Everyone gathered round in admiration to look. There were pearls looped round it and a big flashing green stone in the centre front. Anthony Wan was fingering it and prancing about, really pleased with himself.

Malcolm looked away and his insides churned with strong feelings. He hated Anthony Wan for getting all the attention all the time. Although he would never have admitted it in a thousand years, he was jealous. It was just the way some people seemed to get a lot of friends. They got fussed over by their parents and seemed to get friends all the time, as a matter of course.

Malcolm got nothing. He did not feel valued in any way. His dad ridiculed him, his mum was too frightened to defend him and the only queer sort of thrill he got was from bullying kids, making them do what he said, just like his dad did to him.

He watched Anthony being fussed and stroked on the stage and he could have torn off the beautiful sparkling turban and ripped it apart and screwed it in his face. The thought excited him. He could almost feel the material in his hands.

The rest of the school came in for the dress rehearsal. The teachers sat round the sides, the youngest children sat at the front and at the end there was long enthusiastic clapping. After the audience filed out, Malcolm Keen dragged out the stepladder, climbed up and checked the special spotlights. Mr Carmichael saw him and said 'Well done.'

Malcolm took his time. He seemed to be intent on what he was doing as he tinkered with the screwdriver, but his eyes were watching the door leading backstage. He saw Mrs Springfield come out with the carrier bag containing the turban. He saw her go to the big cupboard on the wall of the hall and place the bag inside. He observed that the cupboard was not locked or secured in any way.

'Finished up there, Malcolm?' asked Mr Carmichael, strolling through.

'Nearly. I just got to put the ladder away.'

'Well done. The lights look fine. Come and get a drink when you've finished.'

The double doors at the back of the hall swung closed and brushed each other once, twice. Silence. Malcolm climbed down and crossed to the cupboard. He picked up a black binliner as if he was collecting rubbish. Opening the cupboard, he grabbed the bag containing the turban and stuffed it down into the black plastic.

As he did so he noticed a strong woody smell.

It stayed with him that gloomy November afternoon as he went, foxlike, through the school grounds to the maintenance area on the far side. There he opened the tall slatted gate, let himself into the compound and stood looking at the school incinerator. It was squat and rusty. He had intended to take out the turban and rip it up with force, to release some of the rage he felt.

But there was something different out here. Something slightly creepy.

A blanket of fog had settled quietly over the grounds, distancing him from the warm lights of the school building. In the pregnant silence he had the eerie feeling that he was not alone, that something might be watching him in the fog.

He changed his mind about destroying the turban and decided instead to just get rid of it, that would upset Anthony

Wan enough. That would do for a start. However as he tried to lift the blackened metal flap, to stuff the bag into the stinking body of the incinerator, he had the shock of his life. The flap wouldn't come up. At first he thought it was just heavy and rusted up, but when he looked properly he saw that something was holding it. A hand was holding it down. A green hand with skin stretched between the fingers.

He shouted in revulsion and wrenched his own hand away. In the compound the atmosphere seemed suddenly full of malice. A whiff of rank scorched air puffed at him from the guts of the incinerator. He turned and fled. Behind him the slatted gate stood wide open and the dropped binliner sank softly, folding in upon itself on the concrete floor.

CHAPTER TWENTY-EIGHT

It was the evening of the play. Children were in position inside the doors of the hall. Each held a pile of handpainted programmes fresh from the art class and each had been drilled in what to say by Mrs Springfield. 'Good evening, would you like a programme?' And *smile* she said. Don't glare at them, *smile*!

Now Mrs Springfield bustled into the hall in her good dress. 'All set now, everyone? Don't forget ... be *welcoming!*'

Outside the doors the hubbub of queueing parents grew in volume. The ushers fingered their programmes and waited. Mrs Springfield strode to the cupboard on the wall and opened the door briskly. She stared at the empty shelf and frowned. The bag containing the Caliph's turban had gone. She was momentarily baffled but then her face cleared. Someone had probably taken it backstage. Someone trying to help. A slight flush of irritation rose up her neck and coloured her cheeks. Why did people meddle? She knew exactly where everything was, why did people have to come and interfere?

'You can open the doors now, children. Open the doors, let them in,' she called as she hurried backstage.

Her consternation grew as she studied the orange faces lined up in front of the mirror. Arrested in mid-application of their exotic makeup the company peered back and shook their heads.

'What, my mum's turban gone?' asked Rufus.

Mrs Springfield nodded.

Anthony Wan looked in dismay. His parents were in the audience. He could imagine his father seated, waiting, clad in his best business suit. The regal turban made such a difference to Anthony's performance. Knowing he looked so good in it gave him the confidence to stand up and say the lines. He grew increasingly anxious.

'Well, has anyone seen it? Anyone at all?' Mrs Springfield's voice was exasperated. 'It can't have just disappeared into thin air!'

Mr Carmichael was seated in the corner. He was staring at the floor, considering who could have taken the turban and why. At last he looked up, scanned the room and found the face he was looking for. He held Malcolm Keen in a long look. Malcolm stared boldly back and did not falter.

Anxiety settled over the cast. Time was running out.

Rufus was relieved to feel a small push in his side. He excused himself quickly, got up and went out.

'Has anyone taken it for a joke?' demanded Mrs Springfield. There was an anxious silence. Everyone was proud of the hat.

'Might the cleaners have taken it?' asked Sarah Day. She was dressed in her spangled Scheherazade costume with a ruby affixed insecurely to her navel. A string of pearls circled her head and formed a loop on her forehead.

'They don't ever go in that cupboard ...' Mrs Springfield shook her head.

Nick Diamond appeared at the dressing-room door. He was stage manager and was giving the calls.

'This is your five minute call. Five minutes to curtain up, everyone.'

This prodded Mrs Springfield into action.

'Well, we have no turban it seems. We will have to improvise. Sam, run to the kitchens and get some tea towels. As many as you can find. Be quick.'

'Yes, Mrs Springfield,' said Sam. He jumped up and made for the kitchens.

Anthony gazed blankly at his hands. A deep sense of shame was spreading over him. Tea towels. He would have to go out there with tea towels round his head. He would look a complete and utter fool. His father and mother would see, would hear people laughing at him, their derision. He felt sure Malcolm was responsible and turned his brown eyes on him sadly. He did not understand why Malcolm hated him so much. As Mrs Springfield started to pin tea towels feverishly around his head, Anthony watched Malcolm. He saw the triumph in his glittering eyes, sensed the exultation beneath his blank controlled face.

'This way, Rufus!' called the Nubbler as they sped through the school grounds. It was dark and there were stiff dead plants in the gardens.

Rufus was holding on to the small green hand. 'This is scratching my legs!' he gasped.

They screeched to a halt. 'You'd better hold on to me, then. Hold on tight!' decided the Nubbler.

Rufus put his arms round him and they started to run again. Then suddenly they were not running any more, but floating over the spiky bushes and wintry beds. Rufus held on tight and his heart soared. The Nubbler could fly! He could even fly! They floated lightly down over a hurdle fence on to the concrete beside the incinerator.

'Here, quick!' said the Nubbler, holding open the black bin-liner. Rufus yanked his mum's white bag out of it and put his arms round the Nubbler again. They bloomed up over the fence, levelled out and flew back to the school building. Rufus's clothes undulated in the cold wind. He laid his face against the Nubbler's leafy scales and held on tight. They landed lightly on the tarmac.

'Go! Go quickly!' the Nubbler urged.

'Thank you! Thank you!' Rufus shouted and impulsively planted a kiss on the Nubbler's long face. He ran in through the doors and pelted down the deserted corridor.

Anthony was standing before the mirror. The tea towels looked absurd on his head and he wanted to die. Anybody could see they were tea towels. Mrs Springfield had stuck some stupid brooch on the front. She had taken it off the collar of her coat.

The door burst open. Anthony spun round with a surge of hope. Rufus stood there with the carrier bag, plunged his hand in and out came the beautiful, glorious blue and gold turban. The pearls chinked. The rhinestone flashed. Anthony wrenched the towels off his head in one contemptuous sweep. Mrs Springfield wordlessly took the turban from Rufus, placed it firmly on above Anthony's radiant face and shoved him out on stage.

'Be silent, you foolish old goat!'

Anthony boomed his first line in an exultant voice. In the audience his father swelled with pride.

Back in the dressing-room Rufus stood holding the empty white carrier bag. 'I didn't take it, sir,' he said.

Mr Carmichael waved this aside. 'Of course you didn't, Rufus. I know perfectly well who took it.' He looked at the empty space where Malcolm had been standing. 'I know who took it and unfortunately I also know why.'

Outside in a dark corner of the playground Malcolm Keen leaned back against the bricks of the school building. His fists were clenched and he stared up at the wintry sky. Waves of applause and laughter radiated out from the school hall and washed over him. How, how had they found it? How had they known where to look? And what was it he had seen on the lid of the incinerator? It couldn't really have been some sort of hand. Could it?

After the play was over Mum stood up to leave. It was the first time she had attended anything at school as a single parent. She noticed other people going home with their partners and felt a wave of loneliness as she picked up her coat and the programme. Dad was away on a trip, so the question of whether he came to the play, and who he came with, did not arise.

Staring unthinkingly down at the floorboards, she joined the queue at the hall doors. She found herself behind Sarah Day's arthritic granny who was holding an animated conversation with a lady of similar age. Progress was slow.

Suddenly she saw a pair of large feet placed squarely in front of her. She looked up. It was Mr Carmichael.

'What did you think?' he asked.

'Very good. I thought it was very good,' she replied.

Mrs Springfield bustled up to Mum. 'Oh, my dear, those costumes, that turban! It added so much to the production!

My husband is looking for you to thank you himself. You *are* staying for coffee?'

Mum had been going home. 'Well, I ...' she began.

'I'll find you one,' said Mr Carmichael. 'Just until Rufus comes. Really, it's the least we can do. A quick coffee to counter the excitement.'

Mum laughed and went with him to the dining-hall.

CHAPTER TWENTY-NINE

A few days after the play, Anthony invited Rufus back to his home for tea. There were just a few school days left before they broke up for Christmas. Rufus accepted, but with certain misgivings.

He was worried that Anthony's parents, being Chinese, would be different and strict or something. He didn't know quite what to expect of the house. He'd been to the Chinese restaurant in town with Dad but the people there seemed very hardworking indeed and far too busy to get to know.

After he had been to Anthony's he felt stupid for worrying. The house was perfectly normal, one in a street of similar houses, they had chicken for tea and watched television and played on the computer until Mum came to pick him up. Anthony's mum had been the only person at home and she was very kind and pretty. She thanked Rufus for being such a good friend to Anthony, for helping him to settle in at school. Her hair was deep black like Anthony's and it shone like silk.

The furniture in their house was different. The wooden parts were dark and ornately carved. On one table, in a handsome pot, stood a miniature tree. It was one of the most lovely things Rufus had ever seen. The tree itself was made of silvery material and on the ends of the little branches polished pink stones had been fixed, like fruits, and were held in place with a binding of fine silver wire. The cool, glossy stones made you long to touch them. They were made from rose quartz in a beautiful candy-floss pink.

Another thing he liked about the house was that outside the kitchen door, fixed to the eaves, was a set of wind chimes. They were silver tubes of varying lengths beneath a little pagoda-style roof. As the wind stirred them they touched each other and chimed in sweet sad voices. They sounded lonely, as though they were far from home.

CHAPTER THIRTY

It was the day they broke up from school and excitement mounted steadily all morning. At midday they ate a vast Christmas dinner and this was followed by the noisy pulling of crackers and hooting of feather blowers. For once the teaching staff suffered the racket in silence, knowing that soon, mercifully, they would be at home on holiday.

In the afternoon a Christmas party was held. It was anticipated with glee by the pupils because an 'entertainment' was always put on by the more rash of the teachers. This could take many forms, and even now rumours were flashing round the school that huge Mr Lyle the PE instructor had been glimpsed while being dressed by Mrs Springfield as an enormous fairy. It was also rumoured that their computer teacher, Mr Clistle, had been seen dressed as a girl in a large gymslip.

Overfed, madly excited about the imminent holiday and all it promised, they surged into the hall for the party. Rufus, Eddie and Anthony scoffed sausage rolls and crisps, and played 'Splat the Rat' where you had to whack a bean bag posted down a vertical drainpipe. It was harder than it looked.

At the end of the afternoon Mr Lyle and Mr Clistle emerged in the much-anticipated costumes to perform a ludicrous play for them all. Mr Lyle as the fairy wore a vast frothy net skirt and little round wings. Mr Clistle played a schoolgirl and had perfected a loud high-pitched giggle which made them all nearly die laughing.

At the end everyone went back to their form rooms to collect their belongings. They staggered off, arms filled with all the products of the term's work. Paintings, calendars, pieces of pottery, Christmas cards and wooden birdfeeders were all borne in the direction of the school gate. In the form room Rufus was sorting through the stuff in his desk when Anthony appeared and walked over to him. He was carrying a package which he held out to Rufus.

'For you, Rufus,' he said with a grin. 'Happy Christmas.'

'Oh! Thanks,' said Rufus, surprised.

'You open it now, see if you like it,' urged Anthony.

'OK.' Rufus agreed and eagerly ripped off the paper.

'Careful, it can break.'

More gently, Rufus unwrapped the present. He took off the final layer of tissue paper and there in his hand was a silver tree with pink stones, just like the one in Anthony's house.

'Oh,' breathed Rufus stroking the stones, 'oh, *thanks* Anthony!'

'This is for good luck. Is also thank you, Rufus. For being my very good friend.'

Rufus stared at the beautiful tree, turning it over and over. He smiled happily at Anthony. Malcolm Keen, who had silently entered the classroom, stood in the background. He watched this friendly exchange and looked for a long time at the little silver tree. He was consumed with envy.

CHAPTER THIRTY-ONE

Rufus walked home through the housing estate, holding the silver tree carefully in his hand. The pockets of his trousers were filled with sweets won in the party games. His sports bag was stuffed with work and paintings and with Christmas cards from his friends. There was one from his form teacher, signed Sean Carmichael. He had given them all one. It was funny to realise that Mr Carmichael had a first name like everyone else.

The evening was growing dark as he wended his way along the pavements, and his sports bag grew heavy. There was going to be a frost. Cold air was descending on to the empty street.

So it was almost Christmas. It would be different this time. He would be spending the first part with Mum at home and the second part with Dad, Eunice and Twit. The truth was he didn't know how to feel about it. He didn't know how he was supposed to feel. Of course it would be nice to be with Mum, and there wouldn't be any arguments or shouting. She was taking him to the cinema twice, she said, to two good films. She always let him have one of the huge buckets of popcorn.

Then he'd be going to Dad and his heart leapt when he

thought of Twit. They'd done his bedroom up and bought the Red Arrows duvet. They were taking him to a pantomime in Cheltenham.

Rufus reflected to himself. Well, it had happened. His parents had separated. At least he no longer had to fear what it might be like. This was it, this is what it *was* like. It was second best, of course, second best to having your mum and dad together, but to be really truthful it was not absolutely *all* bad. There was Twit, all the arguments had stopped, Mum seemed happy and Dad was cheerfully talking about giving up his hated job working for the furniture company.

It still stung him to see his dad so devoted to Eunice. They touched each other all the time. He sensed the grown-up love between them but it made him feel shut out and he couldn't be happy for them. He supposed he could get used to it, but he'd never like it, not seeing Dad and Eunice go into their bedroom at night and close the door on him. He just hated that. Hated being shut out. At home he could have gone in.

On bad nights the Nubbler came. He sat by Rufus's bed and talked to him and then sleep came easily. It was nice that even though he was not in his own bed at home, the Nubbler knew where he was and came to find him.

The sports bag felt so heavy that Rufus stopped to change hands. It was getting dark now and he was cold. The pavement narrowed to a footpath here, moved away from the houses and ran alongside the park and playground. It was edged with bushes and behind the greenery, swings and a climbing frame reared up blackly against the sky. They looked as sinister and unfriendly as a gallows.

In the distance there was a wooden stockade. They played there in the summer, pretending it was a fort or castle, but now everywhere was deserted. He hurried on, leaving the houses behind him. Warm light glowed from the windows as families drew their curtains on the bleak scene outside and settled down for the evening.

Ahead of him he heard a noise. He could see no one but there was a movement in the bushes beside the path.

'Rufus?' said an enquiring voice.

'Yes?' answered Rufus uncertainly.

'That's him, Frankie!' someone spat. It was Malcolm Keen. Two figures came forward out of the gloom. One was Malcolm, the other was Malcolm's cousin Frankie Knotwood. Though only fifteen years old, he was a hulking and notorious bully. Before Rufus had time to think, Frankie had grabbed him by the shoulders.

'We want you, Rufus,' Frankie said in an oily voice.

'Yeah we want you,' echoed Malcolm, 'we got a Christmas present for you.'

Frankie Knotwood clapped a coarse, rasping hand over Rufus's mouth and dragged him out towards the stockade. Rufus was shocked. He kicked and twisted and tried to shout but Frankie overpowered him easily, marching him out over the stiff frosty grass. The sports bag fell from his grasp and his paintings fluttered out over the ground. In his other hand he clasped the silver tree Anthony had given him for good luck.

Malcolm strolled behind, enjoying the spectacle. Frankie dropped Rufus inside the stockade. He tried to struggle to his feet but Frankie placed a large evil training shoe on his chest.

'My cousin says you been annoying him,' he said.

Rufus said nothing. He was very afraid.

'He does.' Frankie pushed at him with his foot.

'Have not,' said Rufus in a small voice.

'Hear that, Malcolm? He says you been lying.'

Malcolm came closer. 'Is he calling me a liar? You calling me a liar?'

'I'm not calling you anything,' muttered Rufus.

Frankie stood over Rufus and he looked huge. His big feet were inches from Rufus's face.

'Get up.'

'What for?'

'Just get up. You'll see what for.'

Malcolm Keen tittered.

Rufus's heart thumped like a drum. He could think of no way out, no escape. Malcolm Keen was in front of the only exit from the stockade. It was almost dark and the place was deserted.

Suddenly his head was thrown back as Frankie bent down, grabbed two fistfuls of his anorak and yanked him to his feet. He felt something click in the back of his neck and it left a sharp pain. Rufus found himself staring into Frankie's glittering, excited eyes. His breath was foul, old cigarettes, stale burgers, dirty teeth.

'Rufus,' breathed the disgusting Frankie, 'Rufus, you gotta learn to do what I tell you ...'

Rufus hung there and said nothing.

'See?' Frankie shook him.

'SEE?' He shook him again, violently.

'Yeah, yeah I see. Look, what do you want?' shouted Rufus in desperation, hearing the break in his voice, hating himself for being so afraid.

'Don't shout at ME, Rufus,' the oily voice reproached him, 'I don't like it.'

'Yeah, you might frighten him,' added Malcolm.

'Yeah, I might get nervous. You ever get nervous, Rufus?'

He shook Rufus again. 'You ever get nervous? You nervous now?'

The two cousins laughed.

'He's got something in his hand, Frankie,' observed Malcolm.

Frankie whipped the paper bag from his hand and drop-kicked it across the grass. It landed with a soft rustle of paper. The silver tree rolled half out of the bag and lay shining on the ground.

'It's what his little friend give him for Christmas,' jeered Malcolm in a scornful voice. 'I seen him, it's pathetic.'

'Yeah, looks foreign to me. I don't like foreign stuff much, do you Malcolm?'

'Nah, gives me the creeps.'

Malcolm suddenly and viciously kicked the tree back towards Frankie. Rufus gasped.

'No, don't!' he said.

'No, don't!' mimicked Malcolm in a high-pitched voice. 'No, don't Frankie!'

Frankie picked up the bag by a corner. The silver tree fell fully out on to the ground.

'Well, well,' Frankie purred. 'Ain't that pretty?'

'Please don't break it!' Rufus shouted but he knew it was hopeless. He was close to tears. He watched Frankie's big black shoe cover the tree and screw it this way and that into the hard ground. Some of the beautiful pink stones pinged out into the grass. Frankie removed his foot. The silver trunk and branches were a twisted mass of wire, ground into the earth. Rufus could not help himself and began to cry.

Malcolm was pleased. He looked at Rufus crying on the ground and felt the familiar pleasant flicker of excitement and power. He looked back at the mangled tree and slowly his face turned white. His mouth dropped open and all the hair on the back of his neck stood out in terror.

'FRANKIE!' he muttered, pointing to the ground, his voice changed entirely ... 'FRANKIE!'

Frankie spun round to look. 'Yeah? ... Just what is *that*?' he breathed.

On the ground a hand was moving, picking up the pink stones. Slowly, carefully, it gathered them up, placing the broken parts together in a small pile. It was a green hand webbed with skin between the fingers.

'Oh Christ, I seen that before!' Malcolm's voice was high and terrified. 'I seen it before!'

'It's like a hand!' Frankie whispered almost to himself. 'It's like somebody's hand! ... It's MOVING!'

'Frankie, let's go!' Malcolm squealed, and he turned to run.

There was a sound, a gasp, a soft, low explosion like something terribly inflammable bursting into flames. Frankie looked up and shouted with fear. Suddenly, shimmering in the entrance to the stockade, stood the Nubbler. He was bigger, much bigger than usual and his skin was flushed pink. A kind of weird light surrounded him. His hands were neatly crossed over his front.

He began to walk slowly towards Frankie and Malcolm. They cowered and jabbered, clutching each other. Suddenly, violently, the Nubbler lashed his tail. It whipped past the cousins, uncurling, and crashed into the stockade. They leapt into the air whimpering. The Nubbler came on, backing them up against the fence. The sound of his breathing filled the stockade. Frankie and Malcolm stopped. They could go no further.

'It was him,' said Frankie in a tiny voice, blaming Malcolm.

The Nubbler's face was inches from theirs. His big eyes

shone and the tufted ears inclined down towards them. He studied them for a minute, his front rising and falling as he breathed. Finally, he extended a webbed finger towards them and spoke in a soft, warning voice:

'Rufus Clark is my friend. I look after him. Leave him alone.'

Frankie and Malcolm nodded frantically, grinning with fear.

Then the Nubbler did something which surprised even Rufus. He took in a huge, heaving breath. His shoulders rose and rose. Then, with a terrible deafening roar he blew out a single, pure stream of fire. He moved his head in a quick circle and the fire whipped up, burning a black smoking arch on the wooden fence all round the cousins. They stood transfixed, holding each other, gazing up at the scorched wall of the stockade.

The Nubbler stepped politely aside. Frankie and Malcolm ducked down and ran for their lives, shouting and babbling with fear. Their feet pounded away over the frozen grass. Silence fell. The Nubbler and Rufus eyed each other fondly.

'How did you do that?' asked Rufus wonderingly.

'Don't ask me to do it again,' said the Nubbler. 'It tastes terrible. Come on, I'll take you home. Your mum's getting worried. Climb on my back.'

'I love you, Nubbler,' Rufus said.

'I love you too,' said the Nubbler. He bent and picked something up from the ground. 'Here you are, don't forget this.' He handed Rufus the tree. Rufus stared at it incredulously. It was perfect, reassembled and shiny and perfect. Rufus put his arms round the Nubbler, his cheek against the leafy green scales. He closed his eyes and held on tight. He hoped if he held on tightly enough some of the enormous love he felt would pass through to the Nubbler and he would feel it too.

Together they went out of the grim stockade, collected the sports bag and its scattered contents from the field, and flew home through the frosty night.

CHAPTER THIRTY-TWO

Two and a half weeks later Christmas was over and Rufus sat on the floor of his bedroom packing his suitcase for the umpteenth time. He looked at the new diver's watch on his wrist, a present from Eunice. One hour until the coach came. One hour before the start of the skiing holiday. He was scared and excited and his stomach had butterflies. Dad had come to see him off and was downstairs chatting to Mum. It was queer to hear his voice filtering up from the kitchen, like old times.

Rufus stopped folding his new ski gear and reflected for a moment about Christmas. Well, it hadn't been too bad. He had gone twice to the cinema with Mum, and to the pantomime with Dad and Eunice. Eunice had booked them good seats near the front and he had even caught some of the sweets thrown from the stage. Someone behind him had lunged for them as they came whizzing through the air, but it was Rufus who caught them.

He and Mum did not, as he had feared, eat a solitary Christmas dinner together without Dad. Instead they went to Gran's house. There was a big family gathering which Rufus didn't fancy much at first, especially as Mum made him wear smart clothes, but once they arrived he changed his mind.

Uncles and aunts he hadn't seen for years gave him presents and one of his cousins called Mike was there. Rufus remembered Mike as a real wimp with a perpetual cold, but he had grown up a lot and improved. He and Mike had been glad of each other, especially when Gran got out her videos of old family weddings and the uncles and aunts started alternately sighing and cackling with laughter.

Rufus turned his attention back to the job in hand. He picked up the checklist from school and carefully placed the things into the suitcase.

The new blue ski outfit, soft and warmly padded. The spectacular yellow goggles with reflective glass so people couldn't see your eyes. Big warm furry boots for mucking about in the snow and the tobogganing Mr Carmichael had told them about. Padded gloves. Blue sunscreen for his nose. His washbag and towels, his money, his passport.

He turned the passport over in his hands. It was the first one he had ever had and this, above all else, underlined the specialness of the trip. It made him feel grown-up. He, Rufus, without Mum or Dad, was going out of the country, on ferries, through France and into the Alps. He pressed the passport between his flat hands and tried to control the rising nerves. He wished the bus would come, that he was with Eddie and Anthony and Mr Carmichael and that it had all started to happen.

The air in the room was suddenly displaced and the Nubbler appeared beside him. Rufus turned to him with relief and excitement.

'I'm glad you're here, Nubbler, I'm getting worried, it'll be all right won't it? I mean, I'll come back? Mum and Dad will be all right?'

The Nubbler came over to him and peered into his face. 'It'll be all right, Rufus. You don't have to worry. Everything is going to be fine. Remember the bit I showed you?'

Rufus nodded eagerly. 'Skiing down that slope!'

'It's all going to be like that. Like that and better.'

Rufus turned back excitedly to his suitcase. He began to wave things in front of the Nubbler. There was so much to show him.

'Have you seen this? It's suncream, see, it's blue!' Rufus laughed. 'I'll have a blue nose!'

The Nubbler watched Rufus with growing sadness.

'And have you seen these goggles? Guess who gave me these? It was Twit! And look at my furry boots, see, they're really warm for the snow, feel inside, it's all furry!'

Rufus held the boot out to the Nubbler but the Nubbler did not respond. Rufus finally saw the expression on the Nubbler's face. He lowered the boot.

'Is anything wrong?' he asked. Unease swept into him. 'You don't look the same ... what's the matter?'

'I've got to go too,' said the Nubbler softly.

The excitement vanished from Rufus's face in an instant.

'What? Go where? Go where, Nubbler? D'you mean you're coming skiing with us?'

The Nubbler watched Rufus with big sad eyes, and shook his head.

'Oh no! You're not going away? You're not going away from *me*, Nubbler?' Filled with anguish, Rufus forgot the suitcase and turned to the Nubbler. 'Don't say it's that, *please* don't say it's that!'

The Nubbler suddenly put his head on one side and

listened. Then he did something which astounded Rufus. He lifted the black headset from around his neck, put it over his ears and looked away, concentrating.

'Oh come on, Nubbler! Oh please don't do that! Tell me what you were going to say! Don't start listening to music!'

After a little while the Nubbler reached up and pulled the headset lopsidedly off his ears.

'It isn't music, Rufus,' he said. There was something odd about the way he spoke. 'It isn't music. You can listen if you want to ...'

Rufus came slowly over, took the strange black headset from the Nubbler and put it on. The metal was ice cold. Coldness seemed to flow from it down his cheeks and throat and over his chest. His first instinct was to throw it off in fear.

He could no longer see the Nubbler. Everything had gone dark except for a thin rectangular line of light. He realised he was inside a room. A dark room with the door closed. As his eyes adjusted he found that he could make out a single bed along the wall. In the bed was a small, curled up figure. There was a coldness and despair in the room which chilled his bones.

Downstairs a door was violently slammed and a man's voice roared in anger. A woman's voice screamed back. The figure in the bed began to cry in small frightened whimpers. It was a young girl. Rufus could see her hair spread out over the pillow. Violence and fear permeated the whole house. The little girl twisted in the bed, arms round some shapeless toy, her hands pressed tightly over her ears.

In an instant Rufus realised how far he had come, how far the Nubbler had brought him. He had been like that, terrified, listening to the hate-filled voices.

He pulled off the headset, shaken. The Nubbler took it

from him and placed it back round his own neck. They looked at each other. A lump rose in Rufus's throat.

'Is that where you're going?'

The Nubbler nodded.

'Aren't you afraid?'

The Nubbler shook his head. 'No. You understand, don't you?'

Rufus nodded. 'Are you going now?' he asked in a small voice.

The Nubbler nodded. 'Can't leave her like that, Rufus.'

Rufus walked slowly over to the Nubbler, knelt down and put his arms round the fat body and leafy green scales. The Nubbler laid his long sad face next to Rufus.

Rufus knew it was selfish, knew that the girl in the bed needed the Nubbler more, but he couldn't bear the thought of losing him. Hot tears brimmed over and flooded down his face.

'Don't let them hurt you, Nubbler,' he said.

The Nubbler shook his head. He squeezed Rufus with a small green hand.

'You'll be all right now,' he said, 'now you're on the right track.'

Rufus was going to say 'All I needed was a shove' in a brave joky way but he couldn't get the words out. He swallowed wetly.

The Nubbler spoke in his ear.

'All those things I showed you Rufus, they're just a few of the things you can do with your life. It's all out there waiting. The skiing, the diving, Australia, hatching out those chicks and *thousands* more things. You can do them *all*! Join the wreck diving club too. You can trust Mr Carmichael, he'll help you, you'll see a lot of him.'

Rufus said in a thick voice 'But you, where will you be?'

The Nubbler hugged him sadly. His big eyes swam with tears.

'Not far, Rufus. Only on the headset.'

Suddenly from downstairs there was an excited babble. Mum shouted something, laughing, and then he heard Eddie and Anthony thundering upstairs.

'Rufus?' shouted Eddie. 'Rufus, COME ON! How much longer? The coach is outside!'

They burst into his bedroom, hot and out of breath. Rufus was still on the floor. Wiping his face quickly on his sleeve he turned to face them. As he did so, Rufus let go of the Nubbler. He felt the leafy scales pass from beneath his fingers.

'You OK, Rufus?' asked Anthony.

'Yes,' he nodded.

'You're coming? You're coming, aren't you?'

Rufus sat on the floor beside his suitcase. He looked up at his best friends Eddie and Anthony. Out in the street he could hear the meaty rumbling of the coach engine. From downstairs he could hear the voices of his mum and dad as they waited to wave him off. In his back he felt a soft tiny push. He got to his feet, picked up his suitcase and took a long look round the empty room. Out in the street the coach driver revved the engine. Rufus went quietly out, closed the door behind him and walked downstairs to the hall.

Far away in the dark bedroom the little girl stopped crying and turned to look.

'Hello,' said the Nubbler.